fə

LONDON UNDER SNOW

SNOW

JORDI LLAVINA

TRANSLATION BY DOUGLAS SUTTLE

FUM D'ESTAMPA PRESS LTD.
LONDON - BARCELONA

This translation has been published in Great Britain
by Fum d'Estampa Press Limited 2020

001

The moral right of the author and translator has been asserted
Set in Minion Pro

Printed and bound by TJ International Ltd, Padstow, Cornwall
A CIP catalogue record for this book is available from the British Library

ISBN: 978-1-9162939-6-0

Series design by 'el mestre' Rai Benach

This work was translated with the help of a grant from the Institut Ramon Llull.

FUM D'ESTAMPA PRESS

CONTENTS

LONDON UNDER

SNOW

HAND & RACQUET

I first arrived in London on a February day in 2009. I was thirty years old. Among other personal effects, I had a black leather notebook like those that Le Corbusier once used to sketch out architectural ideas or to note down some of his theoretical or technical thoughts. On the second blank page, I wrote a title: "London Under Snow (and other reflections)" in pencil.

Five days before I was to set off for the English capital, a colossal snowstorm had set alarm bells ringing and I was worried that the thick blanket of snow shown on the newspapers' front pages would turn into a terrible layer of ice – I didn't realise that the services in London actually work reasonably well: snowploughs, workers with reflective jackets and armed with spades and salt all work together to remove the settled snow. On the television, Hyde Park was an indistinct, indivisible white, and all of the hated lead-grey squirrels had sought refuge inside tree trunks or litter bins. The typical phlegmatic British character had been slightly disrupted: the special news reports showed images from Chelsea of playful teenagers building snowmen against the snowy white blanket and keeping bottles of beer cool in the midriffs of their creations. They very sensibly buried the bottles deep into the bodies, patting them down well so that only the bottle necks were showing and making them look like penises. There were occasional acts of vandalism: one person smashed a shop window while others were found fighting in the street – their splattered blood casually imitating some piece of Pollock artwork there on the immaculate canvas. Stupendously smart City workers were seen shouting for taxis that happened to be on strike that day and which were lined up along the road. The file of black cabs, the funerary quality so typical of London taxis, in the middle of a mono-tone backdrop of absolute white, lent the scene a dreamlike quality, like something out of a Giacomelli photograph. This was three days before my flight and I wasn't sure if I would be able to go or not. Rather than abating, the storm was getting worse.

I almost called this particular short story "London Under Snow (and other reflections)," deciding to forget the romantic idea of calling it "Hand & Racquet" that, apart from being a title or perhaps instead of being one, would impose itself as one of the revelations of my fleeting trip. This despite the fact that it's quite probable that the twelve or so people who will read this story will rather know it by the title "The Hat." And I don't dare suggest colloquially. Either way, it is neither the time nor the place to spoil the narrative and strip it of suspense.

Just two days before my ticket indicated that I should depart, an abundant rainstorm hurled itself across the city. There was a webcam installed somewhere high up in Trafalgar Square, dominating the space presided over by Nelson and his imposing lions – a little fat for my liking – lying at his feet. Instead of showing a milky layer of snow across the urban epidermis, it broadcast images of the ground awash with water, a grey sea in the middle of the city, London's bread and butter. And while there was still a lot of dirty, residual snow on the motorway verges, hills, in park corners, on sloping roofs, and in the folds of the lead frock coats worn by generals sitting atop their snowy-maned horses, London had gone back to its habitual rough and tumble and I was finally going to discover the city after so many years of waiting. So many, in fact, that it's embarrassing just to think about it.

Perhaps I had already given up visiting, no matter how long I lived. I don't know. It all started when Nacho phoned me. At the moment the phone started ringing – an old model I had bought from the second-hand market in Barcelona before the Olympic games came to town – I was struggling to extract a convincing expression from my paltry intellect to use in my unclassifiable essay on philoso-phical terminology. Ringing and ringing, the phone failed to scratch the surface of my conscience until the twelfth or thirteenth ring; something that my friend sarcastically brought up when I finally answered. Seconds before that, I had been speculating as to whether a language existed that specifically conjugated the subject *God*. I don't mean, for example, "God sees all" or "God knows your heart." What I mean is that *sees* or *knows* are forms of the verb in the third person singular that include every human in existence: masculine, feminine, etc., but who haven't achieved divinity. One thing is a personal verb and another is a hypothetical divine verb. God should be reassigned another verb form. A unique form. Essentially present. A semantic or majestic plural with a singular formulation. I don't know. What isn't right is that it coincides with the personal verb form that is applied to created living beings. If you must know, it was with this gibberish that I was contending when the phone rang, and Nacho began telling me all about his strange trip.

'About time,' he blared. 'I thought you had died. I've only been trying to reach you for half an hour now. What're you up to next weekend?'

My friend is one of those industrious men who tend not to dedicate more than two minutes to each of the things that they deal with throughout the day. This attitude is perfectly illustrated by a gesture that he often repeats: with his right hand open and perpendicular to his body, he hits the table as if his hand were a hammer and the table a piece of meat. He does it several times, repeating the odious mantra *pim-pam* over and over. He matches the *pims* and *pams* with the rhythmical energy of his hand. What's more, my friend knows very well what I do every weekend and with a regularity that does not take kindly to change. I am imperturbable in my habits. I don't do anything special on my Saturdays and Sundays, and most certainly not anything productive. I like to have the whole weekend to do nothing in particular or obviously productive. I would be incapable, for example, of going to the cinema, to say nothing of the theatre. When I speak of a slight modification, I might perhaps be referring to trying a new brand of beer. Going to the supermarket on a Saturday afternoon at half past six, when the rush is over, and happily back at home without bumping into anyone in the street, no cats, no children, no women, can only be undertaken for one thing: thirst. Thirst for alcohol. And then, though you don't exactly know why, you opt for a Czech beer instead of your usual German brand. And you allow yourself a little treat because it turns out that each cheeky little bottle costs an eye-watering three euros forty-five.

'I'm sorry,' I replied. 'I already have plans for next weekend. How are you? All good with the Dominicana?'

The Dominicana was the beautiful girl who, not more than twenty days before, Nacho had shown around the second-hand markets of London.

'All good, yes. So, as I was saying, I don't care a whit if you already have plans. You'll have to change them. Next Friday afternoon at half past one, you have to check in at Reus airport to catch a flight over to Stanstead, a secondary airport about sixty kilometres from London.'

'Don't stress me out,' I said, interrupting him. 'What are you on about? You know that I can't stand it when people try and organise my life. No woman has ever done so in four decades and it's because of this that I can now proudly defend both my personal independence and my more… more… radical freedom.'

As Nacho fell silent it occurred to me to re-educate him in the benign concepts of personal independence and radical freedom. Many years before – perhaps twenty-five or more – we had played on the same basketball team. My position was small forward: he played centre. Nacho was a mostly disorderly player, but he scored twenty points every match – all the more remarkable if you recall that three-point baskets didn't exist back then – and he would go back to the changing room with the same neat parting in his hair as when he had taken off his tracksuit and had started warming up. On the other hand, I was a much more technical player, elegant when shooting, precise in my assists and elusive when one-on-one. But over the two years that we played together, my contribution to the team was laughable: during the second season I spent most of my time warming the bench.

'You're going to go to London: I need you to do me a favour. And it's just not right that in forty years on this planet you've never once been. Jordi, Jordi…' It drove me mad when he would say "Jordi, Jordi" followed immediately by an irritating, expectant silence, a pause that was the equivalent of the phrase: "come on, can't you see that you're an idiot?" 'You'll be at home for a while longer, right? I'll be round in half an hour. Don't go anywhere.'

'Listen,' I said. But he had already hung up. I have never liked people planning my life for me. But Nacho is one of those people.

'It's a Cashmere Gill,' spewed Nacho. 'Tradition and good taste, exquisitely sober, the typical Scottish hat: you couldn't afford one even if you saved all your wages up for three months.' Hyperbole had always been his favourite resource. 'A marvel. A piece…' He paused for a few seconds as he looked for an adequate adjective. 'A piece… not a unique piece, but a relatively uncommon one, you might say.'

Nacho had always been very fond of expressions of social ranking, never once forgetting to remark on social differences in all of our conversations. Anyone who didn't know him might have thought that he was one of that class of men who looked down on you with scorn or disdain or, at the very least, with condescension. He spoke down to you. He put you in your place, as if it were the case that everyone belongs in a certain place in the world – which I doubt.

Though Nacho came from a good family, his father, Ignasi Serratosa, had been bankrupted by a holiday complex on the Costa Dorada that went under hardly two years after it had opened. He had gone to prison because of his shady dealings in the face of the crisis, but was released three or four days later and, having paid a bail of some twenty million pesetas, walked out of there as if leaving Mass or exiting the cinema with his hair parted crisply down the middle and wearing a seemingly freshly ironed between-season jacket. That was in 1988 or 1989 and it was clear from the start that the setback had not affected his family's well-known haughtiness.

My friend dressed his six-foot stature in irreproachable elegance: he wore a hat when no one else around here wore one; or a flat cap like the one he was now holding in his hands, turning it complacently between two fingers. Every season he would visit a tailor, a close friend of the family, who would cut his shirts to size. He was a professional, he had once told me, very old – a kind of emeritus tailor, I thought – on Carrer Muntaner in Barcelona, who would speak with lines of pins sticking out of his mouth while he marked out trouser legs or lapels.

The flat cap didn't seem to me to be unique or that special, though it would seem that within the world of the smartest hats, a Cashmere Gill: the genuine Scottish flat cap, was a classic – his words, not mine.

'Look here: there's the problem. Despite the cost, despite the quality, do you see? There's just an odd… it can't be a defect: it's impossible! The shop has been selling hats to everybody who's anybody for the last three centuries. To the British Royal Family, do you know what I mean? The Queen of England herself wears hats made by the artisan hatmakers at Lock & Co.! But look at it, do you see?'

My friend had gone over to the window and was slowly turning the cap in his fingers, waiting for a beam of light to reveal the defect within the cashmere.

'Can you see? It's like a stain. Very slight, I'll admit. Perhaps not a stain, more like a shadow. Or not even that: the suggestion of a shadow.'

I nodded obediently, but was incapable of making out the stain or whatever it was on the side that he was showing me, though I should mention that I suffer from presbyopia. That said, the impression I got was that the hat was not a miracle of immaculateness in any way. It was the same effect you get when you have a pair of four or five year-old velvet trousers: there's always the one leg a little worn by washing and daily contact; fabric brushed to such an extent it's as if it's been scraped bare. I didn't admit this to my friend, though his disdain wouldn't have bothered me at all. By then, Nacho's shows of arrogance simply didn't affect me. Rather, it was because I didn't feel like wasting my breath on something that didn't really concern me. I didn't care. I listened to him and confirmed what he said, occasionally articulating a tut that reinforced the shaking of my head. It was a little like someone listening to the rain: it didn't matter to me if ten or ten thousand raindrops fell.

In the end, I intervened. 'Yes, of course,' I said. 'Not really a stain, perhaps. A shadow. Or perhaps rather the suggestion of a shadow. Not too much but… of course… if the hat is so incredibly expensive then perhaps you should do something about it.'

Nacho sat down, satisfied. He had said everything he had wanted to. All that was left was to wait the two or three minutes he needed to take the plane ticket and reservation for a three-star hotel in Paddington out of his wallet. The man trusted implicitly in the blind confidence that, one day during puberty, he had decided to place in himself and in his exceptional ability to get himself out of any imaginable situation. With age, his exquisite condition as a man of the world had simply become even more refined.

'I knew I could count on you, Jordi. Thank you. I have already spoken to the shop, Lock & Co. Hatters, on St. James's Street. You won't believe the shop. This is the only way that someone like you will ever be able to set foot in a place like that, you know what I mean? Well, don't take it the wrong way. They say that they don't understand, that it has never happened before in more than three centuries! More than three centuries?! Tradition and good taste, exquisite restraint.'

Nacho often repeated his arguments, littering his long-winded lectures with repeated adjectives.

'They said it has never happened before. Well, there must be a first time, I said to myself. The gentleman who spoke to me on the phone can't have known whether to laugh or cry. He attributed it to an unknown effect that the light in our country has on the cashmere. "Where are you from, sir?" he asked me. "Tarragona," I said. "Tarraco!" he exclaimed, rolling the double r, and exhibiting his knowledge of the city's monumental and historic legacy. He was a learned man; you could tell it a mile away! "What an extremely incisive light you have in Tarragona!" He apologised some four or five times. And his "my dear sir" made me feel right at home immediately. What's what is that next Saturday morning they will be waiting for you to exchange it for a new one. They will offer you some delicious tea and you will eat raspberry jam cakes the likes of which you have never tasted before.'

Lock & Co. Hatters seemed to exist in a world where appointments were still made and nothing was left to chance. Imagine the people, I thought, who must find themselves spellbound before the shop front. And the special few chosen to leave a good wad of cash on the cashier's desk in exchange for the right to take away one of the shop's valued pieces.

I picked up the Cashmere Gill as delicately as if I had in my hands the incorrupt arm of some saint or fragile Minoan statue, while doubting I would have spotted the guilty shadow even if I had run some special detection device to distinguish that which is only vaguely seen across it – any reader half-familiar with those television programmes dedicated to stubborn, rather cinematographic ghosts will know what I'm talking about. Not even had I spent hours doing it.

On the inside, however, was a considerable stain that looked like a spot that had burst without the victim needing to worry about taking off his hat: I applied my butcher's fingers to the small bulge that, as it rubbed up against the crown, I imagined to be rounded and bright, rich with pus, wiping its flaw against the interior fabric and making the wearer's hair nice and crispy. I didn't want to insist any more on the absurdity of an item that I then realised to be utterly unique.

Eight days after the episode I've just described, I flew to English soil with a low-cost airline. The last time I had taken a plane somewhere was in the summer when I had flown to Crete on an organised tour that I regretted booking after the first day. Midway through the trip, I spent a whole day locked in my hotel room in Heraklion – a gloomy, ugly city, populated by dirty men looking not unlike prisoners or pimps – and still recall the three-star Castello hotel's reception boy and his weeping left eye. He was a tall, fat boy, of the kind who seem destined never to learn how to tuck their shirts into their trousers, and was owner of a grotesque beer belly and an old-fashioned salmon-coloured tie that moved of its own accord, seemingly independent of the boy's random movements. The self-imposed imprisonment in my room; the smell emitted by the air conditioning unit; the dust on the bedside table; the crack in the bathroom mirror; and the stickers in the minibar in neo-Greek and English all got ever blurrier thanks to my continued consumption of Raki throughout the day, one of the most tedious of my life.

On the plane that was to set me down at Stanstead airport were two girls who spoke a Catalan from Lleida. They can't have been more than twenty-five years old, but they looked around forty and were seemingly the perfect size and shape for being sat down on a couple of wooden stools in front of some cow's udders and being asked to milk them down to the very last drop of frothy milk. The girls spent a good hour or so polishing their nails so that once they had finished they could put fake plastic ones, as white as a new doctor's surgery, on top of their real ones. Custom-equipped with their accessory nails, they reminded me of birds that I had once seen at a breeding and observation centre for raptors.

I was carrying the Cashmere Gill in my hand luggage – I don't know why I still insist on using capital letters – as I found it horrifying to think that, hidden away inside the stowed bag with my shirts and waterproof, a foldable umbrella and change of clothes, it might be more likely to go missing or end up in the wrong place. Every now and then short articles appear in newspapers about suitcases that were supposed to have accompanied their owners to Australia, but that had ended up, two days later and without explanation, at an airport in Guatemala.

During the flight, I got up twice to open the overhead lockers and grope around for my hand luggage. Opening the zip, and with the other hand inside the bag – wedged between a literary guide to London, my notebook, a folded jumper and a half-full wallet – I touched the shadow-stained cap, thus making sure that nobody had stolen it. Nacho had assured me that the hatmakers at Lock & Co. always sold their wares in elegant white boxes: 'like a bon-bon from the Parisian sweetshop Debauve & Gallais'. But he had decided to keep the box in which the defective hat had first been delivered.

'I arranged my little collection of condoms… and I put them all, one by one, in the Lock & Co. Hatters box. There they are, standing up straight like teabags, *pim pam*.'

Here, instead of placing his open hand perpendicular to his body, he put it parallel to it, the hand moving progressively away from his chest as he classified the condoms in his mind; the sequence of *pims* and *pams* reminding me of an archivist putting his library cards in order.

'What a variety of colours,' he beamed. 'What an assortment of condom packets! I really must say, I think they look just wonderful, what can I say?'

The thing that made me most angry about Nacho's boasts was the wink at the end.

A bus full of excitable Italians and Spaniards took me from Stanstead airport to Trafalgar Square. Outside, the snow piled up on motorway verges and lay-bys was a degraded colour like that of the base of a mountain ridge, it seemingly trying to drop roots in the rotten, damp grass, or in the chastened asphalt.

A group of students from Rome were shouting and blasting the closed air in the bus with a riot of loud gestures and words. A stench of garlic was on the air, and the fogged-up windows only reinforced the sensation of olfactory oppression.

The hotel was a simple establishment in the heart of Paddington. The road, one hundred metres from the tube station entrance, was blocked off by roadworks and metal barriers that forced pedestrians to take detours.

The girl on reception spoke a strange English. I clocked her immediately: she was from Galicia. My room was number 112.

The key was solid metal, and a worn, dark silver colour.

It was very cold in my room. Very cold indeed. I looked over to the heater hanging above a little desk that sported a lamp and a rectangular cushion of black leather on which you could write letters to your loved ones or complaints to the hotel management. The heater display showed 21 degrees, but the room was nowhere near that temperature: it was 11 degrees at best. I pressed one or two of the buttons before deciding that it was probably best just to leave it.

Putting my suitcase and bag on the bed, I took out the hat and left it on the desk in the middle of the black rectangle like someone planting a bust on top of a tailor-made plinth. The duvet was an ivory bone colour, and there were a number of stains that were a lot more visible than that which was presumably ruining the outer part of my precious cargo. The shadows are chasing us, I thought, and I was in the middle of composing a sophisticated reflection on this when my phone rang in my jacket pocket. On the screen I saw the name of my friend and sponsor of my trip to England. At that moment, however, I was in no fit state to answer, as my sophisticated reflection was carrying me away to a distant memory, to a poem by John Donne, "A Lecture Upon the Shadow": "We do those shadows tread." On the wall near the ceiling, the wallpaper had bubbled up from the damp and a little further down there was a new shadow, made thicker by drops of a sooty substance, as if behind the bedroom wall there was a working coal factory furnace. I opened the suitcase to distract myself from the brigade of shadows and stains that were surrounding me. The poem by Donne, if my memory serves, finished with these two terrible lines:

Love is a growing, or full constant light;

And his first minute, after noon, is night.

I felt rather, but not yet completely, wretched; and these emotions projected me into the bathroom. Before sitting down on the toilet, I was unable to appreciate the scandalously low level of care put into servicing the room – the half-finished toilet paper and the toilet itself without its plastic covering with the usual sanitary advice, printed in two languages on the plastic – as I noticed that something between my forehead and nose wasn't quite right. I felt a light dizziness and rising bubbles of blood, and only had time to quickly rest my elbow on the basin before my nose started to run dark red and I tried to stop the haemorrhage with some toilet paper from a half-consumed roll. My mobile made a double beep to herald the arrival of a message. I threw my head back and pressed the paper hard against my nostrils. It had been years since I'd last had a nosebleed. Perhaps even since I used to play basketball when, so as to strengthen my weak physique, I would exercise my arms by passing a medicine ball to a gym monitor at the beginning of each training session. My nosebleeds back then had more than once made a terrible mess on the court.

It was half past seven in the evening and, between the wearying rush and absurdities of my journey, I had completely lost my appetite. I took hold of the bedsheet, pulled it down and got into bed without undressing. I didn't even have the energy to brush my teeth. I turned off my mobile and must have fallen asleep immediately, perhaps dreaming of an army of stains wanting to devour me or of a hotel that collapsed and suddenly transformed into rubble around my bed. I can't remember.

The next morning, I ate breakfast at the hotel. All of the waiters were Latin American and served the guests with a certain forced care as they asked for the room number or answered queries in their guttural, American English. The other employees seemed also displaced, perhaps feeling uncomfortable in their uniforms or missing the sun of their native lands. A very fat English woman was carting around dirty towels while shaking her head at the situation, as if someone had intentionally made them dirty and she was now forced to take them to be dry-cleaned. The green apple I took from the buffet was tasteless, like one of those wooden fruits used in advertising. On the table next to me a man was reading *The Times* while using the tip of his knife to break up the unbuttered toast lying on his plate. I found myself staring for a while before the man turned to me and smiled apologetically – though I had been the guilty party – before pointing his large, parrot-like nose towards the newspaper, enraptured by the international politics section. Embarrassed, I opened a little packet of freezing cold butter that was incredibly difficult to extract without leaving part of it stuck to the silver paper. When the girl asked me if I wanted tea or coffee, I quite rightly chose the national drink.

The Galician from the afternoon shift was no longer on reception but had been replaced by a freckled ginger-haired girl who, based on my knowledge of accents, had come from either Wales or Sweden.

'How do I get to Hyde Park?' I asked.

'Oh, it's very close, sir. You see?' she answered.

The girl unfolded a map of London on the table and marked the location of the hotel with what could have been an asterisk or a pointy cross. From her squiggle, she drew out a route using arrows. The park was, in fact, almost next door.

There was the threat of rain and I entered the park just as the first few drops began to fall. But it wasn't bad enough to stop my walk. If the timid drizzle looked to be getting worse, then I would find shelter in some doorway or under a tree. Dressed in blue or grey tracksuits, lone runners ran through mud left over from the snow a few days before. Some covered their heads with their hoodies. At times, a dog off its lead nipped at their heels. One could write a whole book about the lope and arm movements of those joggers. There were also cyclists following a specific, well-signposted route. One of them had a lead knotted around the handlebars connected to a dog that was trotting a few steps behind his rear wheel. A pair of boys were passing a rugby ball between them. One of them was the spitting image of Tim Buckley – had I had a camera to hand, I'm not sure I would have been able to resist taking a photograph for a hypothetical report on doppelgangers titled: *Jeff Buckley's Father, Alive; Rugby Ball in Hand*.

Squirrels worked to predict walkers' movements and would approach them in the hope of gaining a nut or piece of bread as a reward. I had once heard that four lads from Liverpool had posed right here in the park for their *Beatles for Sale* record cover, but the record's arboreal reference had by then completely disappeared, and the background was now indistinguishable – be it Hyde Park or the gardens of the Villa Borghese. I felt vaguely emotional thinking about the photo session that took place four years before my birth, and I was immediately reminded – when my mind formulated the syntagma photo session – of the protagonist from *Blow Up*. Were the park scenes also filmed here? No, they couldn't have been; I would have known. Either way, the park in the film was more intimate than the one I was visiting now, umbrella-less and without shelter in the face of the drenching downpour from both the sky and my own mini story. A postcard with an image of the Serpentine that I had received from Marta in the mid-eighties came into my head with an unexpected forcefulness. My memories of The Beatles and Antonioni were, up to a point, logical and followed a pattern, but that of Marta – how many months, years had it been since I had last thought of her? Coming from somewhere that, in one of my more soul-searching meditations, I had once called *The Tomb of Memories*, an overflowing mausoleum from which too often impish flames rise to subdue our cheer, the thought of her expanded centrifugally and completely took over my consciousness with fragments of days long since forgotten.

'Excuse me. Where is the Serpentine, please? Which way?' I asked a man of a certain age. He wasn't running or cycling or walking a dog but was carrying a bowler hat in his hands with a devoted respect and a tenderness he might have dedicated to hair from his dead wife's head, still warm and recently cut, as he wrapped it up and placed it on a veneered base with the honourable intention of leaving it in the vitrine of memories and family heirlooms, of trophies and most valuable medals in the living room of his house. It took me five minutes to reach the lake.

Some immense balls of dirty snow – the accumulated residue of several days of convulsive weather – looked like sculptures of meteorites dotting the tarmacked paths. A layer of snow that hadn't yet completely melted away, lying there on top of a flowerbed like parchment mimicking a Manent poem:

The melting snow is a white
geography: islets, continents.

My mobile rang, the catchy melody rudely interrupting my obsession for metaphors and literary references. It was Nacho, and again I didn't pick up: Marta's ghost was becoming even more untimely than the irritating ringtone. I was reminded that I had two unread messages.

I had already passed up two opportunities to visit London before this trip. So many years later, the two previous occasions were not so much mere possibilities to visit the city on the Thames, but genuine opportunities to have lived a different life. Like the Frost poem, I had chosen one of the paths, and now lived alone; spending my Sundays writing sad, obsessive stories about grey individuals. My Saturdays were spent reading detective novels and watching Premier League football matches on the television or occasionally struggling my way through a philosophical essay that I would never publish. I would ingest the contents of various half-rusty tins with illegible labels that I would serve up on a plate with a fork. Tuna, bonito… even sardines in brine. Gluttonously, I would soak bread in olive oil. I was not a health nut when my diet was concerned.

The Serpentine now in front of me didn't look anything like the postcard my friend had once sent me. It must have been 1986 or 1987. The first thing I noticed about the girl's face – the girl who sent me the postcard – was her hair hanging down across her forehead and eyes. Moving her long, wavy hair out of the way, her eyes would appear with all the beauty – or ferociousness – of a wild savage lit up suddenly by the headlights of a car on the road on a dark forest night. When not adorned with glasses, all eyes look quite naked. Those, though, looked both stark naked and respectful. And not because they were more bulging or rounded than most eyes that I saw around school. The other thing I remember about her body was the scar she had just above her hip, next to a much smaller and more recent burn mark she had got from an iron. It was as if, sooner or later, the scar wanted to close or swallow up the burn mark. She had lived for many years with just the one kidney and was such a skinny, weak girl that her scar was out of proportion with the rest of her body, verging on immodest. As though someone had set a painting of a sea creature (the shape of the burn, with an added beak) in an oversized frame. An empty sea – no boats, buoys, jumping fish, rocks or waving arms – and a passe-partout beach. I'm not sure if the similarity is all that fortunate: what I mean to say is that the girl's scar was two or three sizes too big and should have been four to five centimetres shorter.

She was the first girl to be naked in my bed, and the first one to make me realise that each body has a different taste. That the internal chemical processes produce external results that are not related to the skin. There are some people whose skin smells of well-worn leather. Others of freshly cut wood. There are still others who smell rather disagreeably of straw that has been left out in the rain and sun. Or of iron. I have made love to girls who smelled of iron. I once licked the sex of a girl called Alicia that showed – think a sommelier's spiel – notes of asphalt mixed with overripe apples.

Marta's skin smelled of grass and her hair of lavender, I think, or rosemary. Perhaps it was the shampoo. But it can't have been, because it always smelled the same, even when her hair or skin were unwashed.

She had gone to London to study English. It must have been during our second year of sixth form and she had gone abroad for the whole course. Not long before she left, she wrote me a long letter that I kept for a few days in a little brass box along with some other keepsakes from my school days that, were they to resurface (who knows where that piece of paper might be now), would hurt me a lot more now than the first time. The letter would now represent the exhumed script of a girl who had once loved me, of a person who, dead for the last twenty years, had been kept alive in my memory as a virginal, ever youthful, uncontaminated figure. She had never suffered the impurity of money and never had her hands been wrinkled by time, mounted by over-polished nails and covered by rough sandpaper skin. The letter said that she'd like to "try it" but didn't say anything else. She told me about her imminent trip to London, but also mentioned that, on her return, she'd like to see me and – written again – "try it". She didn't specify whether it was to try going out together or try something else together. Just "try it." Because I was, she continued, a "special person".

I ignored her allusions and I don't think I wrote to her once all the while she was away. She continued to write me letters, along with the postcard of the Serpentine that brought about this digression. So, many years later, I still can't remember her surname. Was it Alemany? Almirall? Albornà? Memory fails.

She came back a little early as she was sick, having first fallen ill the year before she went to England. One morning, a year or two later, I bumped into her, shaven-headed and all, on Carrer Moliner in Barcelona. Her head, significantly smaller without her hair, had taken on the beauty of a walking stick pommel. It reminded me of a bird, beautiful and strange. All of her curls, right down to the very last one, had disappeared. I kissed her on both cheeks and she seemed happy to see me. Only a year had passed, two at most, and we had lost touch. We went to get a bite to eat at a restaurant nearby and halfway through lunch I had the gall to ask her why she hadn't called me since getting back to Barcelona – this after I hadn't replied to a single one of her letters. She told me about her illness, but more so about the wonderful things from her London trip. A few months after our chance meeting, a friend gave me the news: Marta was dead.

'The small girl with the curly hair who studied with us at secondary school, do you remember? I think you had something with her.'

I had had something, yes. This despite the fact that, in the end, we had never got round to trying it.

Her Serpentine postcard was pinned up on the corkboard in my study. It had been there for years, probably from the end of the eighties. Typically of me, I only fell in love with her once she had been buried for a few months – Pere Quart's verse, tragic and ominous, springs to mind: "my dear Marta, dead". Shut in my bedroom, I looked again and again at the photo of the lake: the reflection of the sun on the silver water, a woman with a pram, the back of a towering young man, the subject of the photo, shielding his eyes from the sun as he waits for something in front of the Serpentine. Perhaps he was waiting for a dolphin, or a spurt of water like that of Lake Geneva. I couldn't say if he was also looking at the drinks stand at the very edge of the card. The image was straight out of a Henry James novel.

I spent many afternoons in my room, winding my way through the fabric of my thoughts, regretting having ignored Marta when she had challenged me in one of her letters: "Let's see if you ever surprise me and one of these weekends you come and visit me in

Camden Town. You'd like it". Let's try it, she'd suggested before flying off to London. More than twenty years ago. 'Why did you have to die, why?' I asked myself at the top of my voice, two years after she had come back early only to leave forever just a few months later. Shadows, again. I, who didn't go through the process of the illness, the operating theatres. I, who never accompanied her anywhere. Why did she have to die? The girl it had occurred to me to embrace. My studies started to go downhill and my closest friends weren't able to ease my pain. The girl I had made love to was dead. If anything like this has ever happened to you, you'll know what I'm talking about: my first love, now in the ground.

One night I dreamt that I placed her body on the frozen surface of the Serpentine. It was around dawn and there were no wardens. The bus drivers were yet to sit down on their raised seats and take their wheels, and the ticket collectors were still to start ripping their way through the stubs at the entrance to the park. She was completely naked and the scar on her side was beginning to peel away from her skin, the skin itself getting smoother, like before they had opened her up, as if the scalpel had never entered her. The scar, skinny like an eel, lay on the blue-rock bed and started to dissolve away like water, leaving no trace. Once she was laid out on the ice I went back to where I had come from and, from behind the kiosk in the postcard, I pulled out an ancient wooden chest. With my two hands tightly gripping the handle on one of the sides, I dragged the chest along the muddy path with the intention of leaving it next to the corpse. I asked a barefoot man dressed as a royal guard who the girl was lying out there on the frozen lake, with the sly intention of distancing myself from her. The chest suddenly opened, and the wind blew all the yellow pieces of paper and clothes through the air and across the park and the sight of these things hurt me deeply.

I said that I fell in love with her when she was already dead. But it's more likely that I magnified what the girl had represented during a short period of my life, and that I'm getting confused. Knowing myself well, the most probable explanation is that I'm trying to shield myself from my friend's death. To shield myself from the world. All my life I have relished being a loser. Within my soul, there is an unhealthy tendency towards self-commiseration. Allowing myself to delight in my losses, I have inundated myself with inertia or inaction.

The girl's surname now comes to me: Albertí. Marta Albertí. 1968 to, perhaps, 1989.

I was starting to like London. But what had I come in search of? I had been sent on a noble mission to exchange an expensive hat – by now, most probably frozen stiff in the cold air of my hotel bedroom – at an ancient, venerable shop near Trafalgar Square. Were we to suppose that the cashmere of which it was made was as sensitive as still-warm human skin, not yet stripped from the body – please allow me a doff of my cap to the artistic ambition of local villain, Jack the Ripper – then I don't doubt for one second that it will be frozen through, awaiting the arrival of its friend and owner to remove it from its icy hell; longing for someone to put it smartly on their head, that the warmth of their body might help to thaw its freezing fibres, that the tickle of their follicles might heat up its sleepy, stiff belly, its rigid sides, clenched tight like a mouth in rigor mortis.

London was starting to offer me up its charms; the same ones that I had turned down at least twice before 2009, but I was sure that the objective of my unexpected trip was not just to exchange a piece of apparel. There had to be another, hidden reason. A real reason, I thought, for my last-minute jaunt, as I headed off towards Notting Hill to see George Orwell's old house. There, I would acquire a bag tough enough to protect my friend's hat for when I took it to

St James' Street. It was half past eight on Saturday morning, and the temperature on a thermometer hanging up in a pharmacy window was disconcerting: one degree above freezing. I had hoped to get to the hatters' at around eleven o'clock and so I still had a good hour and a half to experience Portobello market's "incessant tingling, colourful transit of people" – I quote my guidebook and its enthusiastic descriptions for each of the city's tourist attractions. With any luck, I might well get to where the author of *Homage to Catalonia* had once lived, but time was tight. At twenty past nine, I would have to make my way back to the hotel to pick up the hat before taking a taxi over to Lock & Co.

After the market stalls dedicated to antiques of dubious age – printing cases and lead or wooden moulds, glass flasks cracked and clouded by time, rude paintings that would have been unwelcome hanging on the walls even of dust-filled attics – there were those that dealt in sporting paraphernalia: footballs and rugby balls of waxy leather imitating more ancient examples. The owner of a franchise of sports bars had told me, not long before, that from time to time he would go to London to pick up golf clubs, bats, stumps and cricket gloves; tennis racquets with heads that were much smaller than today's, seemingly brandished by Ilie Năstase as a child, to decorate the toilets of his establishments. He would pick up medicine balls and basketballs too, even antique motorcycles from back in the day to ennoble the wall next to the bar, giving the place a distinguished, museum-like feel. Nearby were stalls, populated by sixty-year-old-plus characters with ashen hair, that had been consecrated within the cults of pop and mod: street signs with Beatles album names, posters of Jim Morrison, LPs by The Jam, CDs by Happy Mondays. After them came the antique book shops. In one of them, I acquired a postcard from the sixties of an old pub in Covent Garden that reminded me of something – probably a scene from some film. It cost me £2.20. Further down the road were the fruit and veg stalls. From a rosy-faced old woman in a woollen hat I bought a carton of fresh figs for £3.50 that looked like a box of sweets. Figs in February: where have you ever seen that before? In London, of course, in the middle of the Portobello market on a magnificent stall with its wares so well turned out that it looked like a Florentine stationery shop.

After one hour, and a run-of-the-mill cappuccino from one of the innumerable Café Neros, I went back to the hotel to get the hat so as to accomplish, once and for all, the mission I had been assigned. The sooner I did it, the sooner I could relax. The two figs I ate on my way back upset my stomach a little and while it would have been easier to blame my slight indisposition on out of season fruit – the juice of which had not blended well with the difficult digestion of the milk in my stomach – I've since realised that it was more likely to be that which I discovered on crossing the threshold of my hotel room. I don't mean "opening my room door", because a member of the staff had already done that.

It's difficult to describe what I saw in front of my open bedroom door on the first floor. The stairway stank like a badly swept chimney, and the lift's metal door howled horribly. All of it: the Filipino girl pushing the cleaning trolley; her colleague busying herself from one end of the corridor to the other; the cold kettle and empty bottle of bourbon on the tray in front of room 115; the window with its flaky frame which opened onto the desolation of an interior patio where a washing machine was whirring with an abusive hammering and a student's drum set was beating out a rhythm; all this can be more or less defined with words found in a dictionary. But what I found sitting on the desk in my recently desecrated room, cannot. Or perhaps it can, because in reality I am about to. But I'm not sure I can do it justice. In an exceptional bid that will by no means create a precedent for any future books, I asked my editor to include a colour photograph to illustrate the tragedy. But she said no. She maintained that a photograph would be unjustifiably strange in a book of short stories such as this one.

'What's more,' she said, 'why just one photo? Why not a photo for each of the stories? One for "My Andalusian Cousin", for example. Why not? It might be nice. A taste of the times. Or a portrait of Amat. We could consider it.'

I cut her off.

'No, there's no need to supplement the text with images. I want the reader to form their own image of Amat, with the minimal description I provide. No, no images. Adding images would be like… like removing the soul from the literature. My stories have no need of any photos. And if they don't achieve with words what I want them to achieve, well bad luck. Imagine trying to draw the woman from the story about the dead daughter. Not even I know what face she has. All I know is the lost look of panic and alienation on her face as the emergency services come to take her away. No, it's a bad idea, believe me. It was just a suggestion. An exception. Anyway, I suppose the budget doesn't run that far.'

'It has nothing to do with that, Jordi,' she quickly replied. 'My only concern is the quality of the book. I would never argue with you about even the most expensive rights for a cover picture. Never! You should know that. I haven't pushed anything like this. But, inside? Inside the book, Jordi? It would look very strange… just the one…'

'Yes, yes. You're right. Very strange indeed. You know what, let's just pretend I never mentioned it.'

Despite all this, I still think that a good photo of the scene of destruction awaiting me in my room – disrupting a good part of my Saturday plans – and of the consequent call to arms that it had produced amongst the nervous hotel manager, another man dressed in a grey jumpsuit taking notes, and the chambermaid changing the towels, wouldn't have been a bad thing at all.

The manager – seemingly in shock – wore a golden name tag on his breast that showed his "-son" surname. When he saw me, he took me by the forearm and started to apologise profusely. Having presumably been informed of the disaster by room service, he was visibly flustered, but had clearly been bred for the job: he didn't stop speaking for a single moment as he received me at the doorway to the room. It's quite possible that he had already been there for a while, standing nervously and hopping from one foot to the other. I looked in the room and couldn't believe what I saw.

'The hotel is very old, sir,' he said. Yes, I thought, I had picked up on that the moment I had walked in. 'And, very occasionally, flaws such as what has rather unfortunately happened in your room, luckily while you were out, disturb the peace and tranquillity of the establishment and, as such, cast an entirely unwarranted shadow across its good name and reputation. A name and reputation that have been happily intact for more than seventy years, I might add!'

I have tried valiantly to reproduce the man's discourse as well as my memory allows, with the added difficulty of having to follow his British rhetoric. My eyes were bulging in disbelief and my English found itself stuck somewhere at the back of my throat. In fact, I couldn't help but notice just how poor my command of the language was: I needed to protest, to shout, to chew out some meaty swear words, but nothing came out. You won't get too far with nothing but the word fuck and its long list of derivatives: the acceptable fucking and the inadmissible motherfucker. In my defence, there wasn't a section in my travel guide for insults and swear words.

The heater in the room – yellow or olive green in colour – with the illusion of its red digital numbers, the little grill on its underside, its four black buttons, two of which were stuck down by some grease that had solidified next to them, and the ancient, half-torn or badly torn sticker about something to do with the IRA – I didn't understand the phrasal verb from the slogan – the heater, as I was saying, had dispensed with its elevated position and had crash-landed on the desk. On the wall, in the space that the green box had occupied until not too long before, just below the threatening damp stains, the painted paper had been obliterated by the force of the collapse. You could even see a little of the red brick of the wall, darker in colour than those we use in our country.

The hotel manager had quite rightly decided not to touch anything until the occupant of room 112 had come back. In these kinds of things, the British really are very scrupulous, regardless of whether it's a dead cyclist in Piccadilly Circus – one must wait for the arrival of a judicial officer – or a heating system that has disintegrated on top of a hotel desk topped by the modest coaster – modest in terms of its size, I mean – that happened to be a genuine Cashmere Gill cap. Now I really do intend to maintain my capitals: almost as a posterior homage to a very special item of clothing – over which until very recently sat the slight, almost unappreciable shadow of a defect – that was destined never to reach its final destination on St James' Street. An item of headwear that, in all likelihood, would end up lost among broken umbrellas or mixed up with vinyl records from God knows when and the discoloured, crumpled pages of some pornographic magazines on an old market stall, crawling with fleas and bedbugs, in one of those public markets that show no respect for, or interest in, a hat with an enormous rip alongside other rather evident signs of damage that had disfigured it entirely. It was a hat that, apart from its auspicious origins, was as of that moment not much good for protecting one's skull from the tedious Atlantic downpours or the blazing heat of the Mediterranean sun.

I asked the manager to stay right by my side and then used the hotel room telephone to call Nacho's mobile. I got his answering machine.

'Please, call me as soon as possible. It's very urgent,' I blurted.

A few seconds later I called again and this time he answered. He was very laconic.

'I'm in a meeting,' he whispered. 'You're not angry with me, I hope?' I heard him trying to stifle a snort of laughter. 'You have to understand that I did it all in the name of our friendship, Jordi. I have to go now. Send my regards to my beloved – here, again, was the muffled laughter – Cashmere Guilt.'

I found myself more disconcerted by this than I thought I would be, and attributed his mysterious words to some sort of hidden code that the two messages he had left on my mobile would help me to untangle. But I needed to tell him that his hat had come off rather badly in an unfortunate accident, and that I wanted to put him through to the man with the golden name tag so that he could explain and confirm my complete innocence of it all.

The open grill on the heating unit had made a large cut on the inside of the hat and a constellation of wallpaper confetti now adorned the desk around where the broken heater lay. On the black leather cushion in the very middle of it all, was a piece of cashmere ripped from the hat that seemed to have tried, unsuccessfully, to escape the merciless slab from above. As I was looking it over and about to burst into tears of distress and defeat, the manager told one of his assistants to lift up the unit so as to better evaluate the overall effects of the catastrophe that, apart from the damages already mentioned, had led to two thirds of the hat being liberally crushed. Left speechless, I could feel my arms starting to twitch as if they were about to reluctantly lift me up and away from the room, from Paddington, from the yellow fog of London, from the British Isles themselves. Something had to be done. Storm clouds were gathering and the situation was taking on a bleak aspect – my grandfather, in his own, histrionic way used to say that a lot: a bleak aspect.

In my nervous state, I found myself pulling a piece of cardboard out of my anorak pocket. It was the postcard I had bought from the market, rolled up like a cigar. Other than being framed, it was now unlikely ever to recover its former splendour. I unrolled it and looked at the image and, though having been bought that same day, was incapable of remembering which pub it represented, and so I asked the manager if he knew. As I was asking him, it occurred to me that I hadn't bought the upmarket carrier bag in which I wanted to transport the valuable effects from the hotel to the hat shop. And then I remembered poor, forgotten Orwell, too.

'It's unmistakeable: the Hand & Racquet, a pub of noble tradition. Would you like me to tell you how to get there?' answered the manager, cheekily jumping on the chance to change tack from having to continuously apologise in the name of the hotel.

I was married for ten months. Her name was Anna Descalç. She was an adorable girl who, once together, revealed herself to be intolerably over-obsessive and was constantly washing her hands, and I don't mean in a figurative sense. Anything that she touched would send her rushing off to the bathroom to run her hands under the tap and scrub them with a block of soap for a good minute or two. It didn't matter what: the dishes when laying table; the door handle; even the sofa. It included any foreign object and anyone else

– me, for example. She eventually got to the point where touching the soap was too much for her. Her hands were red and raw while the skin from her wrists up was a milky colour. One morning, before work, I couldn't take it anymore and so I accompanied her to the doctor's surgery where we started our obstacle course by which we tried to cure my wife's illness. In the waiting room, sitting there with an unhappy look on her face, her back as straight as an arrow, I was able to examine the hands which – in or out of the house – she would so very often cover up with gloves of which, obsessively, she had a huge collection. They looked like two red raw little mice, one sitting on top of the other.

Her illness led us to a long, onerous, and unexpected court case. She claimed that her suffering was 'because I had been harassing her from the very first day of our lives together'. I didn't notice anything strange while we were dating, though of course, I did notice her slight untowardness when it came to kissing each other on the lips, and her dislike of holding hands. When we found ourselves back at her flat, the sex was generally fine and, at times, even moderately wild. Two years later, the judge declared me innocent, but by that time I had lost three precious years of my life, a great deal of hair and, in terms of marriage, had suffered from consequences that one day or another I'll have to put to rest in a book. But that is, as they say, another story.

During my two and a half days in London I contemplated my life, not to the extent of looking at the existence of someone else, but perhaps rather like gazing at something from afar. Something, without doubt, well known, but that had lost its influence or, at least, had lost its way and that no longer had the capacity to move or oblige me to live my life to the full or, contrarily, to make me suffer and not allow me to stop until I'd gambled all my belongings away. I was reminded of a delicious line by Sherwood Anderson – or was it Scott Fitzgerald? – that described the sight of a train in the distance as if it were a toy. It perfectly describes that which I found happening to me: the jolt of the wagons loaded up with various, randomly stowed goods with robust wares alongside more fragile ones, the din of what I imagined was the locomotive of my existence whistling proudly – or perhaps a little more faintly, depending on the time of my life – and filling the sky with smoke, the fierce grinding of the iron wheels braking against the tracks from time to time… I was a toy train, malleable tin and sad, feeble wheels screeching like the miaow of a new-born kitten. I had wasted away my youth, running, rather, that little toy train up my forearm and onto the crest of my shoulder before carrying on up the steep scruff of my neck, like a funicular railway, so as to reach the top of my head: a slight shiver as the wheels ran across the skin, and the emotion of reminiscing about so many things that one might have considered to be long dead and buried!

In 1999, I had had my second opportunity to go to London. But like the first, I had declined.

I took the Cashmere Gill and dusted it down carefully. Though it still held its characteristic shape between the loose fibres of the ignominious rip, the calamitous depression of the central and rear parts and the other smaller injuries meant that it was ruined. I left it on the bed, eyeing it suspiciously.

'It's not mine,' I said to myself. 'This is the real problem. And you know what? It was horrifically expensive!'

I arranged with the manager that, once calm, we would try and figure out a solution acceptable to both parties. For the time being, though, reception would give me a key to one of the suites on the third floor, and they would take care of the rest. The staff would move my luggage and all my belongings up to the top floor of the hotel. As he told me all this, the manager's gaze fell for a moment on the violated hat and I hurriedly picked it up and squeezed it between my hands. I was about to say that the dead little creature was mine, but I refrained from doing so. It must have been a reflex action, like when you get back home after a two-week holiday and discover that you had forgotten to turn off one of the bedroom lights, and so you rush to turn it off as if a couple of seconds less would make much difference. The guy in the boiler suit took the heating unit away. He was chewing on a piece of pink gum that he inflated into small, disgusting, saliva-filled balloons.

'Go off to the Hand & Racquet,' recommended the manager with the aim, I supposed, of removing me from the scene so he could make a few phone calls and start to tidy up a little. '*Buena cerveza, muy buena cerveza,*' he said in particularly crude Spanish.

I got the feeling that he was abandoning his conventions, and I had the troublesome sensation that the duty he had shown with a certain efficiency during the previous fifteen minutes – that of a manager truly invested in the wellbeing of his clients – was nothing more than a brilliant, but deceptive, act. Whichever way you look at it, his job as manager of a hotel as decrepit as that one must have included, contractually, the use of all manner of apologetic excuses for the unfortunate incidents that most likely befell the establishment on a weekly basis, fruit of the age of the building and the somewhat relaxed maintenance work of its staff.

It was half past ten on a foggy Saturday morning and Nacho was still unavailable. He would kill me. He wouldn't have any right to, as I wasn't at all to blame for what had happened, but he would kill me all the same. And what's more, buying a new hat – 'you could never afford it on your wages,' I remembered him saying, more or less – was completely outside of my scant possibilities. I didn't know why, but something made me go looking for the pub from the postcard. By then, I didn't have anything to lose as the reason for my journey in the first place had now been horrifically crushed: oh sad hat, what a most miserable end! More than losing it, it had been destroyed, smashed into pieces under my very nose. I would dedicate the rest of the day to walking around the Metropolis.

I first met Anna Descalç on a spring day in 1999 when I was working in the archives at the Biblioteca de Catalunya. At half past eleven I went out to grab a bite to eat, planning to have a big breakfast and so be able to skip lunch later. It was during this that I bumped into her as she was buying the microfilm of some book. The woman at the desk was telling Anna to sign up for a membership card and had given her a document with the registration instructions for the card and the library rules, but she said that it was impossible because that very afternoon she had to go back to her village.

Goodness me; when she dug her heels in about something, she could be as stubborn as a mule. Her face was pretty, though a little too small, and she would flick her long, straight hair up and away from her forehead in a flirty, almost teasing way. It was a gesture that, many months later, I came to see as having all the mechanical ugliness of a tick: she did it constantly, especially when she was nervous. Writing this now, I should admit that her flicking was once an elegant, seductive habit, a very feminine infatuation of hers, but that it had, over time, become unbearable. Of course, in reality, the Anna flicking her fringe away from her face in front of the library receptionist was the same person who would do the same thing in the midst of our interminable fights. Hers was a tormented conscience that expressed itself in her obsessions and ticks: ever opening and closing her hairclips or wrapping her hair bobble around her fingers. For my part, I bend my fingers back and crack my knuckles.

Had it not been for my big breakfast, we would never have met, and I remember my first impression of the nervous girl arguing with the woman on the loans desk. I remember what I said to her as I tugged on her sleeve so she would turn away from the woman and how I gave her a little wink and proposed that which had occurred to me in a moment of impulsiveness that I'm still not fully able to explain.

'Listen, sorry,' I stuttered. 'You aren't… didn't you start a philosophy course at the Universitat de Barcelona?' With this said and out of the way, I was able to get her to follow me a few metres away from the desk and so tell her my plan.

We had lunch together and, in the afternoon, I would borrow the microfilm using my membership and the familiarity that being a veteran of the library meant was conferred on me. I would then either take it over to her in her village or we would arrange to meet in a neutral place.

It was beyond mad. And especially because a few weeks before some good friends had given me a flight to London for my thirtieth birthday that left the next day.

'Now that you're thirty,' the envelope said, 'it's not acceptable for you not to have visited these kinds of places.'

I now realise that had I gone to London ten years ago, my life would have been quite different. Wandering down Charing Cross Road on my own or leafing through old volumes in some antique book shop in Cecil Court, I have no doubt that the microfilm would never have reached its destination, that London would have cooled what I have now come to call the impulse and, as a result of this cooling, or the necessary ripening, if you want to call it that, I am certain that my conscience would have achieved some perspective and the impulse would have melted away as it rightly should have. Of course, I won't ever know and so can only occasionally fantasise about the idea, but on that spring afternoon it seemed very clear to me – yet another example of my total lack of clear-sightedness when it came to tackling the mysteries of seduction and the heart's flights of fancy. Perhaps I would never have ended up trying to untangle a heart as turbulent as hers, embittered by rancour and by a toxic family… perhaps. Nor, perhaps, would I have fallen out with two friends who couldn't understand my last-minute change of plan and refusal of their gift. I had exchanged a weekend in London for a foundational Saturday with Anna, laying the foundations of the bitterness that was to come to the fore during the last year of our life together. Perhaps it's also because of this, or mostly because of this, that I had never visited the English capital until the hat episode.

We arranged to meet that Saturday, though I was yet to get my hands on the microfilm.

As mentioned above, we were married for ten months, but before that we dated for a year and seven months. Throughout this time, her obsessions seemed under control, or perhaps it's just that I was so in love as to be blind to them. That said, I remember starting to get annoyed at the way Anna would criticise my appearance, forcing me to dress properly (at times, tucking my shirt into my trousers herself) or insisting that I wipe my lips where my coffee had left a slight dark mark. At other times, froth from the milk in my coffee that got stuck on my nose or a little bit of mud on my shoes meant my appearance wasn't up to par. It's surprising the things that can turn married life into an unending hell.

It had all the characteristics of a squalid, dark little bedroom. From where I found myself standing, it was impossible to tell if there was a window or sad little porthole to help spread a little light around a space that reeked of stale air. Nor was there any door to a toilet or bedroom to been seen. I was completely alone and, such as the little space was, I would not have been at all surprised to discover a mouse on the scrounge for a morsel of mouldy bread. I supposed that cheese was a delicacy somewhat unknown within the four walls of that particular study. Slap bang in the middle of the room was a wood-burning stove with a saucepan sitting on it that, without having to investigate further, I immediately assumed was empty. I heard footsteps, but they came from outside, and I occasionally heard a detestable melody from a mobile phone or phrases in English, German names and even utterances in Japanese. None of them, however, was able to invade the intimacy of my shelter. Behind the stove was a reversed painter's canvas that was markedly bigger than that which I would have used to represent the scene I was contemplating. With nothing showing but the wooden frame on the ochre underside, there was no way of admiring or criticising the quality of the painting on the other side. Next to the canvas was a flowerless earthenware jug. I particularly like jugs without flowers and I'm also fond of abandoned wreaths left on the backs of bulrush chairs, the stalks drying out, the leaves wrinkling, and the petals withering without the nourishing effect of water.

How the stove and saucepan, left there for want of a table, fascinated me! I imagined the shadowy broth in the squat, rounded pan, a delicate chiaroscuro there in the bowels of the container, created by the painter's brush. I looked closer at the lower, drawer-like part of the stove, reddish as if the flames themselves had branded it – in this case then the pan most likely did contain something or other as it would mean that someone had left it there to heat up and not, as I had originally thought, just to keep it from sitting on the floor. Had there been any room to walk around the miniscule studio, I don't doubt for one second that my feet would have kicked up clouds of dust that had accumulated in the piece and had helped age the canvases (that which I could see, and also the others that I assumed were piled up somewhere else, out of my field of vision) through a kind of natural sfumato, only more intimate. I would have liked to have been able to take a broom handle – my hand resting at the bottom of the pole, just above the brush itself, like someone brandishing an oversized sword – and to have gone around probing the corners of the low slung ceiling to catch splendid examples of spiders entombed in their webs.

I had been wandering around various rooms in the National Gallery, impatiently admiring half-naked woman and goddesses covering themselves with white veils; generals with implacable sneers; dead animals; temples standing against the backdrop of reverential ruins, etc., countries and geniuses, and famous paintings that I had seen in books. But none of these pieces had grabbed my attention like that little *Stove in the Studio*, by Cezanne, absorbing me for a good quarter of an hour.

With the unfortunate episode at the hotel still running around my head – the squashed, beaten up hat, the manager, the guy in the boiler suit – I felt compelled to go and visit the pub from the postcard in my pocket: its façade seemed familiar and I had the feeling that I had seen it in a book somewhere. When I left the gallery, I turned on my phone and, sitting among three other unimportant messages, I found and finished listening to the two messages that Nacho had left me.

There's no need to repeat what they said. But it is worth noting that indignation and relief don't often go hand in hand – which makes what I'm about to say all the more interesting. At this point, indignation and relief are of equal importance to this story. First, indignation: then, relief. But before both of them comes irritation and an irrepressible anger directed towards my friend: his manner, his way of thinking had left me a mere puppet to his whims. And he even had the gall to laugh about it.

'I'm only doing it for your own good, Jordi!'

What would have happened if I had turned up, as we'd agreed, at Lock & Co. Hatters on Saturday morning with a fraudulent replica of one of their prestigious hats, bought from a measly Sunday market stall in Camden Town? Being on a weekend break, it would have been quite understandable if I hadn't bothered to check my mobile.

But the truth is that he had done it only with my best interests in mind (he repeated this mantra at least three times) and, considering this thought from every angle, I felt calmer every time. I had to admit that the ruse had a certain charm about it. Ha! It was even ever so slightly brilliant. Now I understood why he hadn't given me the cheap imitation in its original box, the bastard! The second message revealed me to be less perceptive than I thought: the label inside the hat said Cashmere Guilt. Of course, I had seen the hat's disgusting inner lining and the worn quality of the fabric, but, distracted by my friend's argument, I hadn't noticed anything untoward.

No, I wasn't angry. Nothing had been lost in the incident at the hotel, and that was the most important thing. And I now felt freed from a responsibility towards the hat that had been forced on me. Finally, I could dedicate what remained of the day to wandering freely around the (for me, at least) undiscovered city. It occurred to me to go and find a garden centre or shop of some sort to buy a small spade or trowel. I wanted to bury the hat in Hyde Park. Before that, though, I took the underground back to the hotel so as to plan the last few hours of my London trip in the calm of my suite. I'd sleep a while, too: after so many emotions, it would do me good. And I still had the Hand & Racquet to visit.

I couldn't sleep. Too much excitement. The suite was in no way cold, and the heating and cooling unit seemed newer and safer than the one in room 112. I left the hotel at a quarter past one, deciding to walk for the next fifty minutes from the heart of Paddington to Trafalgar Square, using up only the soles of my shoes. The London Eye was turning parsimoniously, and the riverboats moored at the piers running down into the Thames spewed out contingents of lightly dressed tourists before swallowing up new ones.

Bloody hell, Nacho!

The Cashmere Guilt was in my anorak's right-hand pocket. No, I wouldn't bury it. On the contrary: I had decided that the item – as false as a forged banknote – would accompany me ever more from that moment on. I might put it up in my bedroom, the rip looking more like an open wound with every passing moment, a wounded heart. The dust would form a patina on the fabric. Lovers, finding themselves in my most intimate space, perhaps staying over until the next morning, would on occasion ask me:

'What's this… this relic?'

'Oh, nothing,' I would answer. 'Towards the end of the eighties, a girlfriend of mine went to London to study English and she brought it back for me, like a souvenir. It's a bit rough around the edges. God, I was really in love with her, but she wasn't interested in me, so one day I decided to take it out on the hat. Poor thing, I used a cutter on it and everything. You see? As if cutting down through the cloth would get me to the flesh and bone of the poor girl's head – the poor thing; given in the vein of purest friendship, all those years ago!'

And so, dear reader, now that you are coming to the end of the difficulties, disappointments and sweet epiphanies of a man in his forties in the English capital, who are you to say that were you to pick this book up again in a few years' time and, certain of your memory, start reading the 'Hand & Racquet' story, you were to sample just a couple of paragraphs from the beginning, stopping at the appearance of the hat, who are you to say you wouldn't assume that, indeed, by the end of the narrative the cap will not have been transformed into an icon thanks to an unfortunate accident, but rather because of the anger that I, the protagonist of this tale, had maintained against a person who had not loved me when she was supposed to? Who is enlightened enough to decree what is true and what is false, what has happened and what hasn't?

At ten to three, after getting lost twice and asking four or five fellow pedestrians how to get to the pub in question, I found myself standing in front of the Hand & Racquet.

I know that were I now to write that, many years before, a pre-pubescent me had dreamt of that pub, you would say that I have painted myself too generously, and that my fiction has seduced me to such an extent that I have ended up perverting my story into a closed, circular shape that doesn't fit too well with the erratic course of the phrases I have used throughout the former part of my tale. But I can't deny undeniably true facts: in this case, facts that are the absolute truth. When I saw it, I was finally able to interpret the dream I had had so many years before, a time before internet search engines, when my only connection to the outside world, apart from school, was a subscription to a magazine called *Cavall Fort*. What could be expected from a boy from a small village, hidden away in a valley, in the Seventies? I had dreamt of that very same blue (or was it brown?) pub, packed to the rafters with rowdy men smoking pipes, their tables sticky from the beer that spilled out of their glasses and where I had bafflingly drunk a hot chocolate. I was some eight or nine years old and was accompanied by my grandfather, a dedicated anglophile who had never visited the island (Joan Maria L. B., 1910-1986). I finished my hot chocolate and left the mug on the bar. But it wasn't a mug, but a pint glass cobwebbed with froth.

The fact that in my dream the pub wasn't in London but rather next door to my house wasn't important. It was identical. I hadn't been able to appreciate it in the photo from the postcard. I couldn't believe the coincidence between the image in my dream and that which I now had right in front of my nose. I understood that, during the next few days, I would have to face up to that vision, that I would have to match that of the dream with its confirmed reality, many years later. And I remembered the story by Wells about the green door in a white wall that opened up onto an admirable paradise, and the protagonist's terrible obsession with finding the door when, throughout his life he had had five or six opportunities to cross its threshold but he had always turned them down, citing various, all far more urgent worries.

The Hand & Racquet on Whitcomb Street was abandoned and closed for business. Its windows were full of dust and fly excrement and the stools were piled up on the tables. Two of the beer pumps were rusty – 'Buena cerveza, muy buena cerveza,' the ill-informed hotel manager had told me. The postman had carried on stuffing letters through the hole in the door. Some of them were wrinkled, as if having been caught unawares by water (perhaps a leak, perhaps a flood) and having then dried out amongst the pile of their younger siblings. By then there wasn't a single doubt in my mind: the Hand & Racquet had been waiting for me for more than thirty years and, weary of my repeated absences, year after year, had, like so many things in life, decided to let itself die.

I breathed deeply and, fingering the torn cloth of the folded Cashmere Guilt I had in my pocket, I felt, in London, happier than I had probably ever felt in my life.

MY ANDALUSIAN COUSIN

My Andalusian cousin is dead. A few days ago, I received a telegram
sent from a post office in the Mexican village where he had lived
since the nineties. It had been sent by a woman with a name that
was almost as pretty as that of the village where she had most likely
spent the last few years of her life with him. I hadn't heard anything
from him for around a decade and a half but, while having had little
to do with each other's life, we were quite fond of each other. There
had been a period when he was still living in Andalusia, before the
rude interruption of electronic mail, that we would write long letters
to one another on a monthly basis. He was eighteen months younger
than me and had died prematurely at the age of forty-five. He had
always had a weak heart and I suppose in the end it had simply
given up the ghost. Perhaps he had led an unhealthy life; perhaps
not. Perhaps he had been zealously – unsuccessfully – excessive in
terms of his health. From what I can remember, Andrés had been a
very reserved boy who was the very opposite of the extraverted, jolly,
and easy-going Andalusian stereotype. I have to admit that the news
of his death didn't affect me too much. It was much the same feeling
you might get from reading a newspaper article about the death of

an author that you had followed with a certain excitement at one time but, over the years, had been neglected to the point that their books had been all but abandoned. Had I been given a pamphlet in the street announcing the death of some teenage romance – Àngels or Ester, for example – I'm fairly sure I would have felt more emotional. In spite of this, I was reminded of the Christmas in 1972 that he came to visit.

He journeyed up on his own by train, throughout the night, with his beige suitcase between his legs and under the watchful eye of a ticket inspector with a hat and uniform. When the smoke in the carriage got too much, the inspector would wave his hand at the boy and the two of them would continue their conversation out in the area by the carriage door where they could breathe more easily. You can almost guarantee that they spoke about football. At half past seven in the morning, my father and I went to what I thought was the only railway station in Barcelona, as if the city were not much bigger than my own hometown and had but one railway station, market, chemist's, church, school and cemetery.

We spoke to my cousin in Spanish. Back then my Spanish was rather less fluent, not to mention haphazard and filled with Catalanisms.

We had an allotment on a plot of land wedged between two old houses on the very outskirts of the village that was looked after by my grandfather. He would ride his motorcycle up there and spend hours digging and tending his plants, especially in the morning. That day, we were three of us on the Vespino. My grandfather rode in the middle, holding the handlebars with his then still strong hands. Andrés sat at the front and I rode at the back, holding on to them both like a pannier. On the way back home, I could smell my grandfather's bitter sweat mixed with the cologne that he had put on before leaving the house; this even with his navy-blue anorak that rustled when he went through his pockets looking for his keys, nail clippers, or pipe. There, I would cut out the odd weed with a sickle and had learnt to wield my grandfather's spade that weighed me down like a dead body as I used its rusty blade to make ridges in the earth. That day, deliriously happy and half babbling with excitement, I set about giving my Andalusian cousin what I thought was a short masterclass in gardening.

'You see? With this tool we do the ridges. Look how thin the handle is, you see? That's from holding it so tight.'

There wasn't much greenery in the allotment in December, just a few lettuces or cabbages, perhaps a few chives. My grandfather might have sown some beans a couple of weeks before and I distinctly remember there being none of the delicious strawberries that would sweeten our palates in the summer. My grandfather suffered from problems with his prostate and a few months earlier they had operated on him at the Vall d'Hebron hospital in Barcelona. He said he still felt strong, but the truth is that he hadn't been the same since. That day, though, I could tell he was happy to be able to show his little agricultural project to the scrawny boy we called our 'little Andalusian cousin'.

My cousin picked up a clod of earth, pale white as if covered by spiders' webs or that morning's half-frozen snail trail, and he warmed it up in his hand. I remember it well: he squeezed his fist tight around the earth and massaged it with his closed fingers before letting the crumbling soil, now fine dust, slowly drop from his hand in apparent imitation, I reasoned a long time later, of an hourglass.

On his first day with us, I helped Andrés to unpack his bag. He would sleep in my bedroom because my sister had declared that she wouldn't feel comfortable sharing hers with anyone else, regardless of who he was and how far he had come.

He unpacked a few pieces of underwear, some velvet trousers with multi-coloured patches sown onto the knees; a pair of well-worn leather shoes, the soles of which had started to yawn wide open; a shirt with a heart-shaped darning on its tails; and a green jacket made of something that my mother called flannel that I'd never seen before. He showed me his wooden catapult and pulled it back for me to see. He also had a handful of fearsome looking, dusty-grey chickpeas in an ancient, transparent plastic bag.

'Ah, I forgot,' he said. 'This is for you.'

I shouted for my parents with unexpected joy. Andrés had brought us a present from Andalusia. "Ruiz Ojeda Hnos. Mante-querías Selectas" was printed on the paper.

'Come on, why don't you open them? said my mother.

It was the first time I had ever tried *polvorones* and, truth be told, I didn't like them at all: they made me choke. I was used to other things such as the oilier Xixona *torrons*, the ones from Alacant or Agramunt like soft little rocks; sweet marzipan; and my favourite Christmas treat of all, crunchy *neules*. But I found those dirty brown little cakes rather repulsive. As I went to eat my first one, the buttery cake fell apart in my hands as I was about to put it in my mouth, making my cousin laugh. But I didn't tell Andrés that I didn't like them. So funny had he found my ineptness as I tried my first one that he then showed us the easier way to eat them. He took one of them, wrapped up in fine white paper bearing the name of the company that had made them printed across a drawing of a tablecloth. It was, if you use your imagination, about the size of a large tea biscuit. He then crushed it in his fist in the same way he had crushed the clod of earth from the allotment, squeezing it so hard that he gritted his teeth. He was a weak boy, much weaker than I was and when he made any kind of effort you could see it on his face and in his body. There was only a year and a half between us, but I could have been two or three years older than him. Expecting it to have turned into a handful of dark floury dough about to fall on the dining room rug, when he untwisted the two little paper ribbons I couldn't believe my eyes: it had taken on the even uglier shape of a dumpling, but had been compacted down and hardened. My cousin was right; it then had a more typical biscuit consistency.

My parents took us by train to Barcelona the next day. Getting off at the Passeig de Gràcia railway station, it dawned on me that the station was different from the one where our young Andalusian guest had first got off his train, and we walked down the most elegant street in the whole city towards Plaça de Catalunya. The shop fronts were all lit up, as were the lampposts, and everywhere there was an air of celebration and festive colours. The kiosks were full of men with hats and fashionable women buying newspapers or brightly coloured magazines and the sound of Christmas carols was everywhere. Further along, we saw some very well-dressed girls, wearing navy blue coats, white socks and ribbons in their hair, walking by with their parents. They looked nothing like the girls from our village; and not even the neighbouring one. One or two of the girls were accompanied by tiny, rat-like dogs wearing clothes that we stared at in shock and we were left dumbfounded when, on Gran Via and in front of the Ritz, we saw a carriage being pulled by two enormous black horses. I don't remember if there was still the Santa Llúcia Christmas market in the square in front of the cathedral, though if there was, then I'd imagine Andrés found the little figures fascinating. Especially the *caganer*, that most Catalan of all the Nativity scene pieces. Though perhaps I'm confusing it with a visit from a few years later, when I was a spotty, red-faced teenager. Either way, one thing I can be sure of is that the four of us – my stubborn sister had chosen to stay at home – made our way down Carrer Baixada de la Llibreteria to Cereria Subirà, the candlestick shop with a stately staircase in the middle of the establishment that I remember sparkling with lights that weren't candles. It must have been a few days before Christmas and, every year, my parents and I would go and buy a few candles to decorate our house with. That year, we were to have a candlelight dinner on Christmas Eve to celebrate our guest being with us. Though, of course, it was the next day, the twenty-fifth, that all of the candle flames would tremble like miniscule palm trees in greeting the arrival of the baby Jesus: the day of broth with pasta, of boiled meatballs served on the side, of duck cooked with plums, of *torrons* and of cava.

The next day, Christmas Day, the two of us were given the job of laying the table while my sister stayed in her room in a bad mood. We performed our duties to the best of our ability. Candles of all different sizes marked the route to the table, running along the sideboard up to the nativity scene we had made in one of its empty compartments where the thin candles stood like funerary cypress trees marking the path up to the cave. My father ceremoniously lit a long match and passed it across the wicks, lighting them and turning them into towering canes topped by torches. We had spent a fortune on ornaments and the two of us rejoiced. Yet just as we were about to eat, Andrés took a deep breath and blew out the four or five candles that were burning next to him. A look, first of surprise followed by disgust, flashed across my sister's face. My cousin wouldn't stop laughing, as if taunting us, and sang happy birthday to you, happy birthday to you over and over again. The joke lasted for some five minutes at least, if not more. He was laughing so hard that I thought he was going to suffocate. Had I acted like that, I've no doubt that my father would have clipped me round the ear and sent me off to my bedroom in an instant. But as he was responsible for my little cousin, nothing happened; my parents smiled at him sympathetically and tried to calm him down. I would have done anything to have had a few handfuls of dirt to throw at him. For those few minutes, I hated him entirely.

A few hours later I was in the kitchen with my mother. I asked her why they hadn't told Andrés off, even if he was a guest, and she told me that she had to tell me something, making it clear that it had to stay between the two of us. It turned out that Andrés' mother, my aunt, had died a month before and, as nobody knew where the father was, the boy would have to go and live in an orphanage. I didn't know exactly what she meant by an orphanage, but it seemed to me to mean more or less the same as a prison and I was left in no doubt that, when my cousin left Catalonia, he would be sent to live in one, something that sends shivers up my spine even today. He had it pretty bad. He hadn't said anything to me over the previous days and I respected that, though it meant it was difficult for me to share in his suffering. Even so, that compulsive laugh and the stumbling way he sang "Happy birthday to you" were seared into my memory like a song of blind pity.

By the third day, we trusted each other implicitly as if we had spent our whole lives together. One afternoon, we were playing cards in the bedroom that I shared with him and my cousin had a pen in his mouth that he was passing from one side to the other as if it were a cigar or stick of liquorice. When the ink burst suddenly, his mouth went blue and caused some vampiric drops of ink to stain his chin. I told him to take the pen out of his mouth and to immediately go and clean up at the bathroom sink. But he didn't seem to mind at all. He didn't move a muscle, the ink mixing with the saliva in his mouth. I was convinced that it would poison him and that we would have to take him to see the doctor who would then send him straight to hospital – most likely in the Citroën GS belonging to the village taxi driver, that also acted as an ambulance – and that there they would not only have to wash out his mouth, but also his stomach. In the end, nothing happened and all he did was drink water until the blue of the ink disappeared and his saliva turned clear again. Nobody else in the house knew anything about it. I just thought that it was an Andalusian thing. Years later, it dawned on me that he had done it to show off in front of his Catalan cousin who, according to him, was a little soft.

Andrés spent five or six days at home with us and I didn't see him again until some years later. After our second and last meeting, there were only the letters that I mentioned before.

The death of Andrés, my Andalusian cousin, has awoken memories in my conscience that are more powerful than I thought. A cousin of mine has died who I hadn't seen for thirty years. In truth, I had only met him twice: the first, over the days that I've just described, back when the two of us were just young boys of nine or ten; and, some years later, the second and last time, when we must have been around fifteen or sixteen. It might have been some fifteen years since I last got a letter from him, written in his slanted, unmistakeable hand, on paper riddled with holes where some letters had been pushed through.

Since then, I have worked as a university professor and have carried out academic research that hasn't led to anything. Nine years ago, I married the most wonderful girl in the world. Two years ago,

I got divorced from the most abhorrent witch in existence. I haven't had children. I take medicine due to a thyroid problem. I follow Barça on the television. I haven't kept in touch with my family. I don't mean my cousin from Andalusia; I mean the ones from here.

I have read a lot of poetry over the years and the laconic, cold telegram sent by the last girlfriend of a taciturn, depressed Andrés with heart problems reads like a poem about love and death. Death, for obvious reasons – reasons that led the woman to send me a letter from the post office in a Mexican village with a beautiful name, like a Cantinflas film. And love, because the last piece of news about Andrés is, without a shadow of doubt, about love. He must have once said to his wife, or friend, or lover, that he had a cousin in faraway Catalonia, who lived in a village with a pretty, difficult to pronounce name. Perhaps Andrés, despite not showing it, thought more about me than I ever did about him. Perhaps, fifteen years ago, he wrote me a letter that I didn't answer and that, a few months later when he was about to write me another, he decided – as we decide many things in life – not to. And so perhaps in that way we lost touch until just a few days ago, when the telegram arrived.

Andrés is dead in Mexico, and I don't feel much pain. It has simply misplaced yet another piece of the puzzle that is memory.

I still have little love for polvorones, despite having tasted some good ones – the patisseries here make them now and they are in no way inferior to the ones from Andalusia. I will never know whether he died peacefully, from a heart attack in his sleep, or in terrible pain in the middle of the day. I don't know if his body will remain in the Americas or will be flown back to Spain. The boy who, in my grandfather's allotment, once crushed a clod of soil in his fist, turning it into a handful of dust, has gone far, even further than Mexico. I doubt that anyone remembers him here, and just a few people in

Andalusia, and I suddenly feel closer to Andrés than to anyone else in the world. But no, it's a falsehood, a trick of memory, a nostalgic mirage. Many years had passed without us hearing anything from each other. And so, people disappear in this way. One year to the next. One decade to the next. For me, my little Andalusian cousin had already started to die many years ago because I had completely forgotten about him until the arrival of the postman the other day, asking me to sign for a telegram that someone had dictated a few hours before, on the other side of the world.

WE, TOO, ARE EXPECTING

As they were having dinner that evening, it started to snow on the television. The woman drew back the curtain from one of the living room windows and looked out at the stain of light coming from a streetlamp in front of the house. Leaving the curtain open, she hoped to make out the first snowflakes before her husband did. It wasn't yet possible to discern the first incipient visual signs, but if she had opened the window, she would have been able to pick up the scent of impending snowfall on the air.

The fresh-faced young weatherman who struggled with his r's had predicted general snowfall all the way down to sea level. The recent images he was commenting on from mid-afternoon that day showed two places under snow: one mountainous, where the accumulation was around eighty centimetres thick; the other was at sea-level, where the flakes were trying in vain to turn the water white. The woman wondered if there was anything more beautiful than snow falling on open sea. In contrast, snow that had fallen on the wharf had settled. As they listened to the forecast, the woman's husband mulled over the lexical metaphors used by meteorologists such as blankets of snow and a sun-drenched sky while chewing grimly on a piece of salmon that had been too long in the pan.

A port worker, getting too close to the microphone as he spoke, said that they hadn't seen snow like this for twenty years. He pointed behind him towards the deck of a little pleasure cruiser that was covered white with snow. Combined with the man's sudden turn, the wind caused some of his words, being too specific and technical for the camera and microphone, to be lost to unintelligible rumour. The woman knew that the snow wouldn't take long to arrive. It might even come that night.

A few hours later, all the roofs and balconies in the city would be white. Just a light dusting; not much. The next day meltwater would run down the drainpipes, fall from the cornices and the streets would be sodden, but all the snow would have gone. The tops of cars and trucks coming down from the village up the road and even further up in the mountains would also be covered in a layer of snow, the windscreen wipers on some of the vehicles still working to clear the last fragments of frost stuck to the glass. Though there is little to melt, it is very cold. But let's not get ahead of ourselves or the story.

Once they had finished dinner, the woman sat down on the sofa and carried on knitting her scarf. Nodding towards the dirty plates, she asked her husband: 'Could you, please?'

She was still a young woman, but her hair had turned grey. She had decided not to dye it, though a dash of colour would have made her look younger and more like her real age of forty-four. The man was reading. He was nearly bald, remarkably pale, and had blond, almost white eyebrows. The lone clump of hair sitting above his forehead served to confirm that he was albino. Even at home, he wore a grey woollen hat and just at that moment he removed it to scratch his head before tapping his fingers on his scalp as if tapping out some well-known song. It was, in fact "Fly Me to the Moon". Though you wouldn't have guessed it from his rudimentary percussion, the song had been running around his head for the last two days. His near complete lack of hair made it sound as if someone was tapping their fingers on a wooden chest of drawers.

The man took the plates off the table, leaving them to soak in the kitchen sink and shook the tablecloth out on the balcony before sitting back down to read at table. Still no snow. He looked up at his wife compassionately (not tenderly, though the two are almost always linked) and watched how she moved her knitting needles while, at the same time, silently moving her lips as if reading under her breath. She couldn't stay still: it was as if she was praying. As if her lips were mouthing the greater meaning of her words. A silent prayer to be heard only by God with his ever-open ears and heart of eternal compassion. She muttered again; knitted and muttered.

'Have I ever told you the story about the Spinster?' said the woman, who we'll call Laura, as she pretended that her only daughter wasn't already asleep: exhausted from her day at school and her after-school swimming class and her maths homework in the evening at her Nanny's side. That she wasn't tired of eating the sinewy meat at dinner time that hurt when she swallowed and bored of the milk that upset her stomach and made her vomit on her pillow. She imagined whispering one of her fairy-tales in her sleeping ear.

'The Spinster, yes. Well, she was a normal woman, a little flabby around the edges and about fifty years old. No, wait! Not flabby. The opposite. She was thin. A bit of a hippy. Had she not worn such colourful jumpers and headbands, she might have passed for a witch. A terrifying witch, oh yes! With her pointed hood matching her bony figure. She had long hair that was so silky everyone wanted to touch it. They couldn't help themselves! White, like…' Here, she turned her head and looked out of the window. 'Whiteish, but not completely white. It was starting to turn white. In fact, now that I think about it, it was like my hair. Hair the colour of ash and cinder because the Spinster never dyed it.'

She often tells the sleeping girl stories in her head. Only in her head and only for her, though she mouths the stories out to give them form. For more than two years her stories have become a muttered whisper which fall into silence as soon as she realises that her husband is watching her accusingly. It's a small wonder that the woman can both knit and tell the story at the same time without losing either yarn's thread. She knows that the girl is sleeping, oblivious to everything, caught up in her dreams; dreams that now and then make her laugh and that occasionally make her shout and sit up, turning on the bedside lamp and calling for her mother, crying out for a glass of water or for the landing light to be left on. She sleeps deeply. Her ear, the one not pushed up against her pillow as if listening out for a heartbeat, is unmoved by her mother's words. Her closed eyes are left unmoved by the shining sparkles of light the Spinster makes as she knits a piece of lilac coloured thread, wielding her needles with the extraordinary agility of an altar boy and his snuffer as the boy reaches up onto his tiptoes to put out the highest candles in a church after mass. The girl whimpers as she dreams and the woman sitting on the living room sofa some ten steps away feels them in her bones.

The woman repeatedly turns to look out of the window; she wants to see the first new snow before her husband does. Lying in front of the balcony door is a wooden clothes peg, stained from use and the elements. Nobody has picked it up to put it back with the others in the little basket or absent-mindedly turn it over it their hands. All too often, fingers require entertainment to shut un-comfortable thoughts out of heads. That said, a clothes peg in hand can also help to bolster, score, and distinguish certain unconvincing arguments or to simply pinch at flesh. No snow. Not yet.

In northern, Nordic countries, the snow in the streets can reach up to a metre in depth. The weather forecast shows the magnitude of snowfall in the north of the continent. Danes, Norwegians, and Swedes don't need to see the snow on television and the woman, who just a few minutes ago had been fascinated by the bare windows on the television screen, marvelling at the thick glass of the window panes, thought she could make out, in one of the images from the report – filmed in the exceptionally cosy, welcoming interior of a youth residence in the Finnish city of Järvenpää – a candle burning between the double-glazed glass. She yearns for snow as she knits her scarf and tells her daughter stories. And she contrives the idea that the Spinster, from behind her market stall, fishes for pieces of wool that are out of her reach with a kind of very thin rod. The woman wants it to snow heavily. She wants the white of the snow to cover up the graffiti of the small dog someone spray-painted black onto a block of flats next to the underground car park on her road a few months before. The spray-paint pup lifts up its leg to take a piss and aims the stream against the lamppost. The unending parabola created the illusion of the dog watering the base of the pole rather than using it as a reference point. As if it were the trunk of a thin, branchless palm tree. She wants no trace of the dog left, to entomb it in the snow.

Silky smooth, white hair; white like the man's hair when they first met.

'The Spinster was running her wool stall at the market. It was the most beautiful and, along with the fruit stall, the most colourful in the market.' She continues the story, continues to knit. The television is off, and the only sound comes from the ticking of the second hand of the clock hanging in the kitchen and the ding of the two hands when they meet at half past. No one hears the falling snow. It is silent, unlike drumming rain or noisy, destructive hail. It is the eye that must notice the snowflakes first.

'But the main difference was that the cheerful, rosy-faced man from the fruit stall had to weigh his wares, while the Spinster sold her wool at fixed prices. "These here cost three for a fiver," she would say. "The ones over there are seven for the little ones." To reach the ones further away, the Spinster used a kind of metre-long rod. "You want some lilac wool, right?" And she would hook the wool up with the rod, as if harpooning a fish eager to be caught.'

The albino's gaze meets with his wife's for an instant. He realises she is muttering, and a worried look falls across his face. About to tell her that she looks like she's chewing the cud, he thinks better of it: the analogy of a cow and his wife's graceful complexion would be too unpleasant.

Finally, he says: 'You look like a pilgrim praying to a holy image.'

The man goes back to his book. He pauses at a phrase by Isak Dinesen that catches his eye: "Martina, who had never heard of wines having names, didn't know what to say". A few seconds later, the woman spots something behind the man and stares at it. She is looking above him, beyond him, as if hoping against hope that snow might start falling from the hallway ceiling. Feeling her gaze on him, he smiles unconvincingly. The woman stops muttering to herself.

The man made a coffee for himself and a herbal tea for his wife and took them both over to the table, moving the plates and glasses that they'd just used out of the way. On the plates were pieces of grey salmon skin and a few bones. At the bottom of his glass was a small violet circle; in hers was a little water. The rim of her glass was dirty as she hadn't thought to wipe her lips, sullied with salmon fat, before drinking from it.

'Could you, please?' asked the woman.

The man nodded his head. He took the plates, glasses, and cutlery into the galley-style kitchen. He didn't wash them, but rather filled the sink up with hot water and soap and left them there to soak, standing the dish from which the fish had been served upright in the sink as it didn't fit, and rinsing it under the tap to remove some of the grease. He then carefully drew up the tablecloth by its four corners, opened the door and, stepping out onto the balcony, shook out a few breadcrumbs and the odd bone. From the sofa where she was knitting her scarf, the woman quickly turned to the window, worried that her husband might see the snow before her.

'Relax,' he said, ironically elongating the word. 'It's not snowing yet. It'll probably start while we're fast asleep,' he said, winking at her.

The woman picked up her knitting needles and her unfinished scarf and started to knit again. Seven years ago, on the first Saturday of Advent, she had bought three balls of wool from the Spinster at the market. All three were of the same colour. And every year, on the 24th of December, she would finish knitting a new scarf for her daughter, leaving it for her at night, unwrapped and curled up like a cat in her bedroom. Seven scarves. This year she was ahead of time: it was already the 13th, Saint Lucia's Day, and she reckoned that she'd have it finished in a couple of days' time. She thought about hiding it so her daughter wouldn't find it before time and every now and again she turned towards the window.

Market day was Saturday. That year, the first Saturday of Advent had fallen on the 2nd of December. The woman wrapped up warm and went to the market. The street was busy: a man was trying on a jacket in front of a stall of raucous gypsies while a girl with a slack jaw tested the elasticity and give of a pair of tights she had picked out from the dozens on another stall. Further down was the fruit and vegetables area: mountains of apples and satsumas; piles of colossal bananas; cauliflowers; purple and light green lettuces; white endives; and an infinity of pointy carrots were all piled up there. Still further away was the churros stall, filling the air with its salty sweet smells. Next to the flower stall at the end of the row was the cheese and olive trailer filled with mouldy blue cheeses and buckets of green, black, brown and claret-coloured olives all of different sizes, some almost as big as plums. They also filled the air with their strong, perfumed aromas. She saw the buckets full of carnations and tulips, asparagus stems to make up bouquets, and cyclamens in plant-pots. She admired the Burgundy red of the pasqueflowers and all the little wreaths of mistletoe, wrapped up in cellophane and tied up with bows, that were sitting just a little further back above two easels. There was also a cigar box where the florist kept her money and some Christmas wreaths with their white, almost translucent berries. One day she had confessed to her sleeping daughter that the berries reminded her of fish eyes.

She didn't stop until she got to the wool stand. There were two women before her, but she ignored them both.

'Those three over there, please,' she said. 'Just put them here.' She stretched her basket out towards the stallholder.

One of the women looked at her disapprovingly and said: 'You're rather eager, aren't you?'

Fortunately, the stallholder was agile enough to serve all three clients at the same time and none of them felt neglected. The first woman gave the other one a nudge with her elbow, but she carried on muttering under her breath, turning her nose up in disgust. The stallholder then turned her attention to the woman.

'You always come just a couple of weeks before Christmas,' she said. 'And you always buy three balls. With three balls of wool... you could make a little jumper and some booties for a new-born...'

'I always make a scarf,' she replied, happy with the interest the stallholder had shown in her. 'Every year I knit a different one. They're all for my daughter: she's seven, now. Seven years: seven scarves. During her first three or four years she was too small to really appreciate them. But now she's seven, she says to me: "Today I want this one, tomorrow I'll wear that."'

She spoke absent-mindedly, and her gaze wandered: she stared at the stallholder's face, and you could have sworn she was staring at the different colours her eyes turned as she moved in and out of the direct sunlight. The woman in front of her in the queue paid and left. As she turned around, she gave her one last glare. In contrast, the woman on the stall was sweet and compassionate. The woman paid no attention to either of them. She was too busy looking for her money to pay for the wool and get back home to start on the scarf. She got so worked up trying to find the right change that she handed her purse over to the stallholder for her pick out the coins to pay for her purchase.

Next to the wool stall was a smaller one that sold reels of fabric. It wasn't there every Saturday and most people thought that both stalls were one and the same. How wrong they were! The girl who ran the other stall had three or four needles sticking out of her mouth as if she were going to sew it shut. Saliva glistened on one of them. Wearing mittens, she carried a steaming cup of milky coffee in her hands, but put the cup on a chair to attend to an old woman who wanted a reel of pink thread, winking at the woman on the wool stall as she told her the price.

The albino recognises the symptoms.

The woman is telling the girl about the day the Spinster had a date with the Weatherman. He took off the suit and tie he had worn to go on the television and put on some jeans and a more comfortable jumper. He changed out of his leather shoes and into some trainers and sprayed some aftershave just below each ear: twice on the right and twice on the left. He then ruffled his hair like someone stripping a tree of dead leaves. He was around twenty years younger than the Spinster and their love was a secret love: had anyone found out about their illicit relationship, it would have caused a scandal. The Spinster, having always lived alone, had even dyed her hair for him. Back at her house, the Weatherman scratched his back with the pointer that the woman used to reach her wool and they ate sushi, drank warm sake from small glasses and laughed. The woman explains all of this to her daughter. She tells her that the Spinster would hide a small television under her stall, that it had a long cable that ran into a socket in a neighbouring bar, and that she'd glance at it from time to time to make sure she didn't miss the daily weather forecast.

'Today, my lover is wearing a purple tie,' she says, smiling.

She is enjoying her story and her lips move faster and faster, shaking more and more frenetically, running around and around, as if controlled by some demonic foreign tic. Perhaps it's the fear of forgetting the story before she's had the chance to tell the girl who isn't there to hear it. The man looks at her occasionally, but she carries on whispering as her knitting gets looser. Withdrawn and possessed by her story, she finally puts her needles down to one side and covers her face. Who knows what bubbles away in that woman's head, just moments before she loses consciousness and falls like a corpse onto the sofa?

The albino goes over to her. He knows the symptoms well

enough.

He mutters: 'Another crisis' under his breath.

He tries to sit her up again but quickly gives up, instead running cold water over a teacloth and holding it hard against the woman's forehead. She regains consciousness and tries to free herself from the pressure of the man's hands and the wet cloth that has started to drip onto her face. She opens her eyes and almost smiles, but a grimace flashes suddenly across her face. She grabs the knitting needles and the half-knitted scarf but doesn't know what to do with them. Who in her position would? She shakes, she screams, she squeezes the needles, point downwards, in her hands and stabs them into the arm of the sofa with such force that it might be funny, were it not so tragic. She then collapses again, this time onto the floor. The man, not expecting such a desperate reaction, doesn't have time to catch her.

That time, two young men came not twenty minutes after he had phoned the emergency services. The nurses unfolded a wheelchair and forced the woman to sit down in it, but she tried to escape from the men's hands and the open chair, albeit without much conviction or force. The second crisis in six months – the third in what had so far been a bad year – hadn't been as destructive as the one before, but there was the intimidating threat of the half-buried needles sticking in the sofa.

Ten minutes after the ambulance left, the man filled a toilet bag with a few things for a night at the hospital. Just before closing the blind to the balcony, he stood on a clothes peg. He looked at himself in the bathroom mirror and saw that he had aged dramatically over the last few days. He went into the girl's room. It had always been empty, devoid of life. The radiator had never been turned on and it was more like a walk-in fridge than a comfortable bedroom. The wallpaper was that of a children's theatre: three elephants – a mother and her two offspring – repeated again and again across a background of palm trees. Only eight years had passed and it was already out of fashion! They hadn't had time to put up the shelves and they sat wrapped up in a corner of the room. The small chest of drawers that was to be filled with the child's clothes and the bed where she was going to sleep after growing out of her cot had been removed as soon as they had found out that the girl was never going to set foot in the house.

Before turning off the lights in the dining room, the albino pulls the needles out of the sofa. They had slumped, and by then they were more docile, about to fall over. He hadn't thought of extracting them when the ambulance had arrived. They remind him of two spears in a bull's back and he laughs at the idea. That morning, he had bumped into his sister and her daughter. He had given the girl a kiss on the cheek and he was surprised that she had asked him how he was.

'I'm good, darling. I'm not too bad,' he replied, tenderly touching her head, wrapped up warm under a hat.

The girl hadn't asked about her aunt, and the man's sister had failed to ask about her sister-in-law.

The next day, the man left the hospital with his hat pulled a little further down on his head than normal. The grey wool covered his albino eyebrows. Ània, his sister's daughter, would soon turn eight. He thought back to the day, then so long ago, when the two couples had bumped into each other by chance in a restaurant. Laura had always shown a certain distain, if not total disregard, for the albino's sister. That they didn't get on very well was obvious, but if they ever found themselves in the same place, as they had that day, they would greet each other amicably. The albino's sister was very pregnant at that time and our protagonist was still yet to start showing her bump.

'By the way,' said his sister's husband, trying to diffuse the situation, 'Happy New Year, if we don't see you.' His wife went straight over to sit down at their table for two, tugging delicately on the arm of her blouse.

'It will be, I'm sure,' said Laura. 'We... we, too, are expecting.' And she stroked her belly, not yet bulging with the foetus, to see how her in-laws would react.

'Congratulations,' said the man. 'We must celebrate.' The albino's sister was, at first, quite surprised. She smiled cautiously and congratulated them on the news but with a sole, inflexible nod of her head, she decided to save the celebrations for another day. Her relationship with her brother wasn't bad, but she blamed the newcomer for the distance that had grown between them. In reality, she took their decision to have their first child at that time very badly. Being of a susceptible temperament, she no doubt thought that the other couple's decision would dilute the importance of the birth of her first daughter. As if they had suddenly created some kind of inopportune, bothersome inquest into the beauty of that period. As far as Laura was concerned, she had always thought that naming a child Ània was one of the strangest things one could do and that, as such, they had done it to remind her and her husband of their own tragedy.

That was all many years ago.

When the man had gone to look for the car to go to the hospital, one or two snowflakes were falling onto the road surface but his wife, lying propped up in a bed, didn't know about it. He kissed her on her forehead. A nurse told him that the sleeping pills had knocked her out in a matter of minutes and that she should sleep for a few hours more, 'until her heart says enough'. After sleeping, a doctor would see her and would determine her state and what should be done after that. Heading up to the second floor in the hospital, the man felt bad that he had seen the snowflakes before her and was almost moved to tears. But he promised himself he wouldn't say anything to her about it.

The next day, the albino left the hospital having slept only three hours on an uncomfortable chair in his wife's room. He needed to go by the house to shower and change his clothes, but he couldn't stop thinking about his wife and her stories. Stories for ears that can't hear and eyes that will never see. The woman had spent the last two and a half years talking to a ghost. She had created a tiny soul through her words. Perhaps the stories had stopped being therapeutic? That morning he would go over it again with the psychologist who had been treating her since the first crisis.

A little melt water was running down the drainpipes. The streets were soaked and all the snow had gone. Time had erased all trace of its fleeting beauty. He thought it much better like this and promised himself again that, should she ever ask, he would hide the fact that snow had secretly fallen on the city that night.

SAN DIEGO, FOR THE RECORD

Ever since living alone, I hang my clothes out on the terrace on one of those portable clotheshorses that unfold like a pair of scissors and that, having always been left sprawled outside, has started to grow ill with rust. Not just the arms and screws; the plastic covering on the wires is also rotten here and there. Never completely empty, solitary pegs hang, pinched or standing upright, on the old wires and, during the hottest days of the year, you might find a spider's web floating in between two of the wings, though I have never had too much trouble with them, touch wood. The pegs, spending all day and night as they do on the clotheshorse and sleeping out on the terrace, have gone from a light, beechwood colour to a browner tone, like varnished oak. I am neither prudent nor bothered enough to put them back in the little basket that I keep in my flat's laundry area where I sometimes leave my dry clothes hanging up on the ironing board for a couple of days: a packet of twenty-four pegs – the wooden ones: I can't stand the plastic ones – costs sixty-five cents. It's not the end of the world and I accept the fact that I have to buy new ones from time to time. I have calculated that a peg has an average life expectancy of around and year and a bit, though there are always exceptional ones that last for a lot longer. Of course, there are some that fall apart and collapse to the floor in pieces: the rusted spring looking like a pair of crotchets going at it; the two twin pieces of wood, dark and tragically separated. Some have to stand upright because their rhomboid-shaped hole is too small to wrap around the wire and so has to squeeze it, putting pressure on the spring, and these are far more likely to break than the ones that hang by the upper, tear-shaped hole between the two matching, inwardly facing, pieces. They fall apart with the smallest amount of pressure. If I remove my clothes as is required of me, then seven or eight pegs are left swinging under their respective wires, the figurative opposite of the swifts that, throughout June, wait patiently up on the pylons, reviewing great distances from their pentagonal watchtower: I have never in all my days seen a flock of swifts that, like unbefriending bats, hang upside down.

All that said, I'm not here to talk about pegs, but rather something completely different. Something quite remarkable, whichever way you look at it – and you will soon be able to judge for yourself.

On Christmas Eve, 2005, I went out onto my terrace with a washing basket full of freshly washed white clothes, smelling of detergent and ready to be hung out to dry. I had run them under a little bleach, something that I tended to do just once a year. There were shirts, boxers, a couple of bed sheets and a nightcap. Please don't ask what a nightcap was doing there amongst the other damp items – there's a perfectly innocent explanation. It must have been around half past eight in the morning. The sky was overcast, but none of the weather forecasts that I had checked said anything about rain. Stepping out, I was expecting to see the ever-present pigeon feathers and their stone-like shit that got everywhere; the unserviceable broom that never moved; the drainage grate that, as ever, had fallen off its perch;

perhaps one or two broken pegs at the foot of the clotheshorse; and the sack of compost and gardening tools I used to plant things. But of all of the things in the world, I was not expecting to find that lying there.

In the middle of my terrace was a soundly sleeping homeless man curled up and abandoned as if he were carrion. As you can imagine, I was rather taken aback.

Standing a little way off, I prodded him, the only result of which was a series of very unpleasant snorts and the readjustment of a body that was lying on its left-hand side and not taking up much room at all. A kind of cardboard duvet, lashed together with string, had moved away from where the man was sleeping and was now stretched out just a few inches from the snoring intruder. What difficulty he must have had, I thought to myself, climbing up to my second-floor terrace with his cardboard shawl, the milk brand it used to encase still visible on its underside, wrapped around him! Bewildered, I tried in vain to remember the phone number for the local police station but had had very little need of it in the last two years and I couldn't remember whether it ended in 357 or 753. Perhaps the situation called for the fire brigade, but which number to call? I could just picture the firemen in the park, shooting hoops and defying the cold in tight, Brando-style t-shirts. Putting the washing basket on the ground and shaking the man's right shoulder, a fetid stench rose up from his body, but he didn't wake up. A few coughs contracted his chest for a moment before a loud burp from his marginally ajar mouth made me jump out of my skin. The aroma suggested that the most abundant, if not only, liquid in his stomach for the last twenty-four hours had been wine.

I decided against tipping a bucket of water over him – too much cleaning up afterwards – rather going for the more melodious technique of a saucepan and a spoon. That got him up, alright. He shot upright, flattened out his food-splattered coat, pushed back the sticky fringe from his forehead and looked at me. He was a good four fingers taller than me and was as skinny as a lamppost under his loose-fitting coat. Though when he smiled I was reminded less of a brightly lit lamppost and more of a rascal who had just finished peppering some windows with stones. Slap bang in the middle of his gaunt face was a handsome, multi-coloured moustache: an authentic, greying moustache with a shade of roasted, burnt hair towards the end that seemed to have come from some scoundrel's cigarette lighter getting too close and burning his face. In a Spanish accent from over towards Portugal, he told me that his name was José Emiliano Flores Mondoñeda and he held out towards me a dark hand with filthy fingernails. I refused, citing the need to hear some explanations from the intruder before getting to know each other.

You might say he duped me, though perhaps my mistake was to let him talk instead of immediately turning him over to the police.

'First things first, Sir. Merry Christmas!' He started up in a flurry of different accents, the palm of his right hand pressed firmly against his chest in the same way that I had seen the Moroccan fruit and veg man, from the shop under my flat, do so many times. This was followed immediately by him folding his arms and squeezing himself tight in the hope of warming up a little. It was very cold out.

'Merry Christmas, yes,' I said, carefully, disconcertedly. 'Merry Christmas? But it's…'

'Can we talk?' he asked quickly.

'But talk about what?!' I stammered. 'But… fucking hell man… You've invaded my space… for all I know this is a house raid!'

'Not so fast, my friend,' he replied. 'I'll explain everything. You'll get it, no problem.'

He spoke slowly and smoothly and didn't appear in the least angry or upset to have been woken up so abruptly. Nor did he seem to be at all bothered by the fact that he had been caught in flagrante delicto inside a private property. Or should that be, in *fragrante* delicto: he stank to high heaven. He was the calmest, scraggiest, most destitute person you could possibly imagine. He wore different coloured socks: the right one was black and the left one a strange shade of bird turd. Of his shoes, one of the soles was more worn than the other, as if he tended to put his weight more on his left-hand side or had a limp. All skin and bone, any kind of shove from me and he would have likely passed out, bashing himself on the window ledge, his neck half snapped on the floor or bleeding out, until that was the end of him. A shitstorm, basically.

But how the hell did he get up on to the terrace? What was going on in his head? How... did... it... happen?

With his open hands facing down towards the ground, he signalled for me to calm down, promising that everything could easily be explained and moving to help me with the basket full of clothes at my feet. Horrified, I refused. The idea terrified me: all of my clean, white clothes being soiled by his fingers, a trail of his black fingerprints wandering across the front of a t-shirt or running over my nightcap.

'Don't worry,' I said quickly. 'I'll deal with it.' Fearing he might ignore me and plunge his hands into the washing basket all the same, images of flocks of injured, filthy, condemned souls and a catalogue of cancer-ridden lungs ran through my mind.

'Relax,' I said. 'You stay there.'

He sat back down on the ground and pulled a stubby cigarette out of his coat pocket before offering to share it with me. I lied saying that I didn't smoke. After that, he held it for a second within the igneous blaze of the blacksmith's furnace that was the flame of his lighter. Once he had clicked the lighter shut, seemingly unaware of the disproportionate size of the flame, he flipped it into the air before catching and showing it to me proudly, exclaiming: 'My lighter, my faithful friend!' The stink of the cigarette was that of burning bushes. Only then allowing him to offer me his explanations, I went about hanging up my t-shirts, one after another, until five of them were fluttering in the air above the terrace alongside the sad, half-folded, bedsheets like damp flags and my underwear, there without the weight of my genitals or buttocks to hold them down. The nightcap was attached to the wire by its tassels like the last piece of a ghost that had suffered the ignominy of being dispossessed of its pallid appearance.

His miraculous explanation lasted the rest of his first cigarette, and the three more that he consumed with an admirable moderation. They came straight out of his pocket – no packet – and though I had long since finished hanging up my clothes, I didn't dare leave the terrace or ask him to cut his story short.

Was I an object of flattery? Certainly, I was. But I don't regret what I did at all. Nor would I know how to justify why I acted the way I did. What can I say? I didn't think about it too much. At that moment, from what I could tell, I had no reason not to trust him and so inviting him into my flat seemed to be the logical next step.

I provided him with clean clothes, shaving cream and a one-use razor, and handed him a pair of clean towels: one for his head and the other for his body and showed him the way to the bathroom, telling him to use it for as long as he wanted.

'Here you'll find some shower gel,' I said. 'And, down there, the shampoo. Right? I don't know how much there is but… just get a good wash, for goodness' sake! Look, take the sponge. You can keep it.'

After about half an hour he came out of there spick and span and wearing an electric blue tracksuit that I hadn't worn for years. The zip running down the front that split the words "San Diego" in two was broken and on his feet was a pair of white trainers. His hair was parted sharply down the middle in boyband fashion and the ends of his moustache looked to have been trimmed, while the two-tone colour seemed to have been dyed uniformly white. He had even put on aftershave from the green flask that smelled like those bags of little sweets, and had placed all his dirty clothes in the bag that I had thoughtfully given him, folding them neatly so that they all fitted in, with the exception of his coat that, following my instructions, he hung up on the terrace railing while I went off into the bathroom to quickly, and urgently, open the window. It was perhaps the first time in a great many months that the poor man had been able to carry out his more basic human functions in a room specifically designed for that very purpose and I didn't dare lift up the toilet lid for fear of what I might find.

'Why don't you have breakfast with me? Then you can be on your way and we can pretend all this never happened, if you know what I mean? But you'll leave properly this time: down the stairs. It will have been an honour to have met you, Mr. Flores. If I can help you with anything…'

His story was still ringing in my ears. What cheek! I couldn't believe it. No, don't you worry at all, Mr. José, I thought as I prepared breakfast. I'll take care of it. I'll lay the table. Ah, the joys of living alone, right? You know what I'm talking about, don't you?

I laid the dining room table with two place mats, some knives and forks, two mugs and some paper napkins before insisting:

'Sit down, please, Mr. Flores Mondoñeda. It's just five minutes. Would you like some coffee? Some milk, perhaps?'

On his mug was the logo of a national newspaper that a few months ago had offered its readers a set of glasses, bowls, and mugs. His tracksuit bottoms sat baggily on his meagre frame and, thanks to a fold on the front, his zipless jacket now read "San ego". Sitting on the sofa, he presented me with a grotesque, denigrated representation of myself just after Birgitta had left me. An oily stain from when I had dropped half a tin of tuna down my front still shone on the lap of the trousers. He didn't look much older than me and, apart from his somewhat moth-eaten appearance, didn't seem to be in bad health.

'I've been coughing up blood for the last few months. My chest hurts and it's as if my lungs are burning. My time's up. I won't live for much longer. I've completely lost my appetite.'

His outrageous story was as follows: he had told me that, as he was now dying, he had promised himself he would reclaim his nephews' birth right, telling me that the place belonging to his descendants was currently occupied by the terrace where, at first light, I had come across him sleeping. According to him, 300 years earlier, his family, the Mondoñeda Arnedo's, originally from the village of Hermisende in the province of Zamora, fleeing as best they could from skirmishes in the War of the Spanish Succession – the fire from the arquebuses, the bandoleers' assaults – had arrived in Catalonia and, having travelled through les Garrigues and under the thick, leafy canopies of the splendid oak forests, had settled in what was now the heart of my little city: right there on my terrace and the adjacent part, namely my flat. He was the last link in the ancient saga – looking at him, I wouldn't have doubted for one minute that his lineage had gone somewhat awry – and it had fallen on him to reclaim the place for his nephews, who were the heirs to the place and all which might have been constructed there some 300 years later. Already supposing that the place his ancestors had colonised so many years ago would by now be occupied by some foreigner or newcomer, he had assumed from the word go that a village or, in this case, a little city would have grown up around the founding nucleus. Likewise, that the streets would be lit along pavements with flattened kerbs in front of driveways, that there would be public squares filled with litter bins, benches and trees, and that spaces with swings and slides would be reserved for children to play in. Of the two nephews, he said that one had run off to Colombia while the other one was a junkie. According to him, those 'damned disgraces' had brought ruin on their distinguished family. At this he appeared to be truly upset, and I thought I saw him almost shed a tear. Mr. José Emiliano, however – seemingly the one person interested in preserving the Mondoñeda saga – had only ever dreamed of getting to know the Catalan homeland of his family and, despite realising that modern law would be unlikely to help, just had to give it a go.

As he unravelled his absurd, serpentine story in his Asturian-Leonese accent, I couldn't help but root for him and his quest. I, who had always slammed the door in the faces of Jehovah's Witnesses and encyclopaedia peddlers, had ended up listening unwaveringly to the poor devil's whole story; this same poor devil who had slipped onto my terrace, risking life and limb by climbing up the drainpipes and along the gutters. Had he fallen, not even the cardboard mattress on his back, folded up like an accordion, would have broken his fall. I found myself moved by the invented farce and his ancient saga, his tall tales about his birth right, and his two absent nephews. When he got to this part, I almost burst out laughing:

'I am the rightful guardian. But you can relax; I have no designs on the place. Nor do I have any children. And at my age… and seeing how my nephews have turned out… well, all the children in the world be damned!'

I planned there and then one day to turn it into a short story. By that point, I was spreading a spoonful of strawberry jam across a piece of toast and thinking about what he had told me before: 'I cough up blood.' He had said it to surprise me, to unnerve me. Again, following my instructions, he had filled up his plate with all of the delicacies that I had offered him. In addition to the butter, jam, milk and cheese that I had put on the table, I had also boiled some rice and fried three sausages, toasted some bread and had produced some slightly stale cupcakes from the cupboard. The man, the penultimate link in his family's possibly illustrious history, sipped at the hot milk in his mug as he told me about his wastrel nephews, the last, lost thread to the story.

'I don't have any children, either, Mr. Flores,' I said as I thought about asking him, though careful not to say it out loud, if he would prefer me to call him Mr. Mondoñeda in honour of his ancestral lineage that today had brought him home.

He pecked at his food like a little bird. Such were the tiny bites of his jam toast that, if the piece of bread had been as thin as cardboard and you had passed it through a holepunch, I'm pretty sure it would have disappeared more quickly.

'Oh, cheese!' he exclaimed, picking up a piece. But he hardly touched it. No, my guest really had lost his appetite; you could see it from a mile away.

'But I don't mind, eh, not having children. I'm relaxed this way, if you must know. But as I'm no trustee for nothing, well… no need for children anyway.'

Were he some highly trained thief, now was the time for him

to pull out his knife and shove it into my heart or neck before emptying my flat of all my belongings. I had lowered my defences, was pouring my second coffee of the day and was confused by the way he would look at me compassionately, even tenderly. Then there was his accent, which was too strong to be fake. If he were acting, then he was doing an excellent job and had most successfully lulled me into a false sense of security and satisfaction at having invited him for breakfast.

He asked me if he could smoke, and I said he could on the condition that he accepted one of my cigars. He bit down on it with his teeth and spat out a mouthful of dry, brown leaves onto the crumbs on his plate. He smoked slowly, from time to time looking at the cigar as he rolled it in front of his eyes, calculating how much of it had been turned into ash. Sitting rigidly on the sofa, and seemingly very conscious of the fact that once he had finished the cigar he would have to leave, his mouth filled with smoke. For many months I, too, had chain-smoked cigarettes into the very same ashtray, lighting the next one up with the burning tip of the previous one. How many years ago was that? If we were now in 2005, then it must have been in the mid-nineties, some ten years earlier. In those days, the tracksuit my visitor was now wearing had already long been out of fashion but, for me, it had been cursed even before. I often wore it at home, but if I ever went out into the street, I would make sure to change out of it and I can't remember a single time that the blue tracksuit had ever seen the light of day, or the neighbours. San Diego – not so much the city, but rather the blessed saint – made me feel deserving of a spark of warmth in my chest from the acrylic fibres of the jacket that I would always wear done up until the zip eventually gave out from use and the spinning of the washing machine.

I lie: it's not true that I had never gone out in my tracksuit. Once, and only once, I had been forced to. It was the time that I had cut my wrists and made a right bloody mess of it. 'Birgitta, Birgitta,' I called out in the same way desperate lovers try to exorcize their ghosts, only to summon more of them, both ghosts and demons, drawing them nearer until surrounded by them, all the while still smelling the girl's perfume throughout the flat, overflowing into our bedroom, and spying in the hallway her woollen hat and keys. Birgitta wasn't there, having only to pass by the flat a couple of days later to pack her bags and leave for good. That day, so many years ago, I vomited into the bath and brought up both my breakfast and lunch. After that, I made my way to the hospital where they sewed me up. It was a ridiculous wound: three stitches and iodine every few hours for goodness knows how long. In the medical report, the doctor in the emergency room had written 'superficial injury' and I, dressed in my stained tracksuit, had insisted that the cut had come from a tin of tuna that had proved difficult to open. I had rolled my sleeves up, so the blood hadn't stained them, though oil had dripped onto my trousers.

The Flores chap, after his rather bewildering entrance, behaved in exemplary fashion. Once his cigar had been turned into three little balls of ash in the middle of the ashtray and I had asked him kindly to leave, as if feeling bad that the visit had been so short, he made nothing of making his way to the door. With both of us smoking away, we could have happily carried on our friendly conversation for longer.

'Don't forget this, Mr. Flores,' and I gave him the bag full of his filthy clothes from which protruded his coat that I'd picked up off the terrace. One of the lapels was turned inside out and now looked like an upturned eyelid.

You might think me a fool, but by then I trusted my companion implicitly. The fact that two hours earlier I had tripped over him on my terrace, like a bullfighter pierced on the horns of some bull, had already been forgotten. We agreed that should he ever find himself back in town, he would pop by to say hello and even though he told me that he didn't have a landline or a mobile, I wrote down my telephone number on a piece of paper that he buried away in his new tracksuit. The story about the Mondoñeda family from Hermisende was already old news and I got the feeling that, had the man told it again, he would have mixed up scenes or tripped over names; the War of the Spanish Succession becoming the American War of Independence or, instead of his nephews, a son would appear in the line of succession.

He told me he usually stayed in charity houses that he came across in the cities on his route, and that he had never gone hungry. But that when it came to sleeping, he preferred to sleep outside.

'The stars are my only bedsheet,' he said, as if having read the line in a poem, perhaps by an Andalusian poet.

'Oh, speaking of bedsheets,' I said, running up to the terrace, 'what about your cardboard?'

'Well,' he replied. 'That's the only other thing I need.' He pointed proudly towards his neatly folded cardboard in thanks.

'Lucky it crossed my mind,' I said. 'The nights get very cold. Aren't you afraid to sleep in the street?'

'Well, I've had a couple of close shaves. Once, not too long ago, some people wanted to beat me with sticks. Another time, they set fire to my socks and burned half my leg: burned off all the hair!'

He offered me his hand, and I took it and shook it hard. I almost hugged him but, having never been a very expressive man and finding it difficult to let myself go, I managed to resist.

'See you around, José Emiliano. I know that this is perhaps not the best way to make friends but, well, if you ever need anything you know where to find me. You have a friend here.'

'Thank you very much for the tracksuit.'

I made a gesture with my hands that meant 'you're welcome' and he smiled gratefully. Off went the tracksuit down the street and into the distance and I suddenly felt relieved to see how the electric blue tracksuit – having come to represent such an important part of my life – was now fading away into the grey horizon of the street. Flores was limping and I noticed he had a slight hunch. His cardboard duvet was folded up neatly against his back like a satchel, and I could clearly make out the brand of milk. Until I couldn't. I had a sudden urge to catch him up and invite him for lunch the next day and found myself thinking about how I'd look up a recipe, cook him duck and even buy some Christmas biscuits for us to share. Some champagne too, of course, and some pineapple to finish it all off. I had never had a vagabond over for Christmas dinner. But I didn't catch him up; I stayed where I was.

Was he a beggar? A charlatan? An angel?

Ten years earlier Birgitta had left me for someone else, and from that day on I hadn't done anything but cultivate misogyny and stop counting.

I decided he was an angel.

No, I didn't run after the angel Flores Mondoñeda. In life, I have long specialised in letting opportunities pass me by, ever stupidly missing the boat and being unable to catch up. I can't remember what I had planned that Christmas Eve, though the Christmas holidays have always been my favourite days of the year and I tend to spend them at home. I like to think back to how, thirty years before, I would spend hours carefully decorating the nativity scene with all of my beloved metal toy cars in neat lines, and how there was always a little one that would overtake the others, skidding around the last curve in front of the manger. A pair of figures would then get out of the car and would dance the twist in front of the baby Jesus. Remarkable things, such as the events that had happened to me in the last few hours, could happen on the 24th of December.

Mondoñeda's story was a fairy-tale, but he was no charlatan; he was an angel, and more specifically the angel I needed, whether destitute or not.

I will never be a believer in all of that fuss about cherubim and seraphim or any other flying personalities in which the North American public might believe. But if you ever have the pleasure of being visited by one of them – especially if they come in the form that mine did – don't turn them away, for goodness' sake. Regardless of the stench of alcohol or state of their clothes. Speak to them. Don't slam the door on them. Flatter them. Don't palm them off with those marzipan figurines that nobody ever wants. Give them warm coffee and Swedish biscuits, the ones that leave a delicate taste of butter on the lips. Cook for them.

I went back out onto the terrace to see if the clothes were ready to come in. They were still damp when raindrops the size of grapes began thundering onto the dusty tiles, like the night, so many years ago, that I had slept in my car as I waited for Birgitta to leave the theatre. The rain had pitter-pattered on the roof of the Peugeot and she had appeared at the main entrance before quickly darting into a car that wasn't mine. And then everything got very complicated, very quickly, and I saw, once and for all, after perhaps five times that Birgitta had made her choice and had left the stage of our two-person opera buffa. I quickly took the clothes off the washing line and threw them onto the bed, damning to hell all the bones of all men who have ever lived, and I prayed that Mr. Flores wouldn't get too wet. Hours from now he would be sheltering under the cinema hoarding or be at the casino café where the waiters would receive his new electric blue tracksuit far better than his old dusty coat.

Yes, perhaps he was now inserting coins into a fruit machine, watched zealously by a sullen Chinese gentleman. An angel in an electric blue, San Diego tracksuit. Perhaps he was warming his lips with a coffee at the bar, running his eyes across the bottles of peppermint liqueurs or the sky blue bottle of gin that looked for all the world to belong in a barber's shop, for use after shaving. Well, at least now he was clean, and his clothes smelled, if anything, of nothing more than an imperceptible mustiness that you wouldn't ever pick up on unless you were standing right next to him. Perhaps he was happily fondling the comforting insides of his new pockets.

I was shocked: one of my shirts had a number of dark marks on it. What had happened? Throughout the first hour up on the terrace and then while the vagabond was getting cleaned up, I hadn't left his side for a second. But – who knows how or when – he had touched the white cotton of one of my shirts. True, his kind's wings tend to be exceptionally clean, but in that dirty shirt I saw undeniable proof of his angelic condition. In the few days before, a number of things had happened in the city: a Father Christmas waving a golden bell had pulled a knife out from under his black belt and slashed a woman's face; while a beggar pretending to only have one leg had stolen some shopping bags and set off at Carl Lewis speeds at the appearance of the police.

But I always get the feeling that, somewhere, there is an angel protecting everyone, and that sooner or later one will appear in an as yet unknown form to bring hope to the world and a glimmer of faith to your heart. Hope even for broken clothes pegs and their rusty springs. Hope even for certified junkies.

All I found to be missing after our meeting were seventy euros from my wallet and my grandfather's gold watch that had been sitting in a drawer and never used except occasionally – on Christmas Eve, for example – when I would retrieve it from its hiding place to gaze at it for a while, stroking the foggy glass that would open up to move the hands backwards or forwards, and holding it tightly in my hand as if it were a magic, energy-giving medallion. The leather strap hung like a squashed worm, dull and worn through years of use. Perhaps I had only been the guardian of old grandad Andreu's watch and now it had finally reached its destination. I'm certain that with a little love and care it would have worked again, although I now remember that it was missing the minute hand. I couldn't quite believe that he had noticed it and taken it away. When could he have done it? It must have been his angelic intuition as he hadn't touched anything else. Or, at least, a superficial check didn't reveal anything else out of place. In the end, the price I had paid for what I got seemed derisory. Like a true believer on bended knee, lifting up their gaze to their favourite image, I smiled a daft smile before, having spent more than four decades as a dedicated atheist, I surprised myself by giving thanks to God and praying that on the next day, Christmas Day, all of the disinherited paupers of the world might, at the very least, receive a serving of hot Christmas pudding with which to warm their stomachs.

A MAN CALLED AMAT

When I got to the restaurant one of the waitresses had just finished mopping the floor. Visibly worried about something, or perhaps tired, the girl scowled. She ignored the fact, though no doubt she knew, that her scowling was very unattractive. She was not what you might call beautiful, but something about her caught my eye. She was small, well-proportioned, and had big eyes. Her hair was unkept and wild and, despite this (or who knows, maybe because of this), was seductive to a fault. Her crimson hands gripped the mop handle and I imagined moving closer to her, picking up the strong, offensive smell of bleach or ammonia. Just the idea of which would be enough put anyone off who might be fantasising about those hands as they served up plates of cloying, mouth-melting foie gras, or a portion of lobster paella. Dressed in a black shirt that had the name of the restaurant embroidered into it just above her breast, she wasn't sure whether or not to put down some newspaper onto the busiest part of the passage that led from the dining room to the kitchen. It was half past five on Saint Steven's, 2002, and the girl opened up a copy of *La Vanguardia* and scattered four or five salmon coloured pages across the damp floor tiles. She did all this with a tremendously furrowed brow. Perhaps she was having a bad day.

'One of the saucepans has just fallen on the floor,' warned the girl, nodding at the floor. 'And this means I'll have to mop up twice.'

Feigning a sudden, rather crude interest in her watch, I moved over to her and, like a choreographer telling a press conference about his most ambitious project yet, gave her a wink and delicately rolled up her left sleeve. I needed only to bend down a little, presumptuously bringing myself closer to her round, cut-glass eyes, and moving my nose towards the hand with which she was holding the mop to pick up her scent. She smelled nothing like bleach or disinfectant and I found myself momentarily imagining her hands serving my table with all of my favourite foods: pig's trotter salad, crispy suckling pig, vegetable lasagne, pumpkin, and bitter orange ice cream. On the other side of the bar a towering waitress was cleaning the coffeemaker and piling all the polished little cups and saucers up on to its silver, mirror-like top. A white cloth was draped across her left shoulder. There were no customers left in the room and the background music was too loud.

My younger brother, the chef, was giving instructions to a kitchen assistant carrying a bag full of a vacuum-packed, orange liquid. As he nodded his head in recognition of his boss's orders, the assistant played with the bag, pinching and squeezing it a little. Had the liquid not been the colour of saffron or apricot jam, it might have looked like a bag full of blood. But I was in a restaurant, not a hospital. A good restaurant, I might add, of which various gastronomic critics had spoken very highly.

The abandoned tables, now waiting to be cleared, were full of dirty glasses and plates daubed with chocolate and sugar grains that shone like crystalline quartz. In the last few years, the restaurant had played host to a councillor; a *député* from the Alsace region in France on a visit to the area; a canon of the church; a Danish actress; and even a drug trafficker. We didn't recognise the drug trafficker until later, when we saw him in the newspaper, handcuffed and flanked by two members of the secret police with their faces blurred out and who were holding him by his arms. The trafficker had left a very reasonable, perhaps even excessive, tip. But that's another story.

Bubbling away inside an enormous saucepan was a broth that, once off the boil, was used to garnish different dishes. In general, a restaurant is a happy place and I saw it in the hustle and bustle of the slightly stressed staff going around cleaning or preparing certain select dishes for that evening's tasting menu, and the newspapers underfoot that spoke of the reappearance of a shady French entrepreneur – and president of a certain football club – who had spent a few years in jail. Restaurants are even happier places on days like these, though the only clues to it being the Christmas season were the little candles burning in the centre of each table. Well, little candles could easily be found on the tables throughout the year – in this restaurant and others throughout the country – but you could tell that it was Christmas thanks to the spiked holly leaves that someone had had the patience to glue to the side of each candle. If you squinted, the leaves looked like the yellow flame's shadow. There was nothing else: no flashing lights, no flowers, no crowns hanging off golden threads, no Father Christmas with his sleigh, none of those yule log figures with their floppy Phrygian hats, and no other such seasonal absurdity.

'Have you had many people in for lunch?' I asked the waitress who had finished organising the cafeteria and started to line up the sundry liqueurs on a trolley.

'Not too many. A table of eight, a pair of lovebirds who complained about the service and a guy who always comes in by himself,' she replied.

I could just imagine the lovebirds holding hands throughout lunch, playing footsie under the table, and muffling a giggle when the leather of one of their shoes squeaked too loudly. I could imagine them complaining about the service: the guy, trying to show her that he's a real man and the girl picking up her glass and holding it in the palm of her open hand as if she were swilling a thick cognac instead of a Cabernet Sauvignon that produces delicate violet tears in the bulge of the glass. All this with little or no decorum and not even the remotest notion of how to taste it. How little elegance and dignity!

I hate lovebirds. But I have a soft spot for men who lunch or dine alone. Having worked as a travelling salesman for three years, I know the type well. I can spot one a mile off, even on their days off, accompanied by their wife and children. I would only need a couple of tiny indications: his arm movement telling his wife and offspring to choose one of the tables in front of them, or his tiny expression of satisfaction at such a welcoming restaurant – a place that he had perhaps discovered in a different life, with a younger woman on his arm and without the children who now crumble bread into the fennel soup with sea urchins served as an aperitif, squirming in their seats and opening cans of orangeade – with such clean, white tablecloths serving food of such high quality. With only these tiny clues I would feel confident enough to say: "That man is a travelling salesman. He might not have his briefcase full of samples with him today, but it's with him in spirit. That's him, and I'll eat my hat if he's not."

'A man who comes every day, even over Christmas? He must be a salesman… or a widower or a bachelor. What's his name?'

The girl shrugged her shoulders.

'No idea. But it'll be in the reservation book. Over there. All I know is that he gave a pathetic tip,' she said, her words dripping with insolence.

I opened the large black book and went to the left-hand page for the twenty-sixth. Written there was: Colomer Presas, 8. And below, Amat, 1.

His name was Amat.

I paused. It couldn't be the Amat that I had known some twenty years before, could it? No, it's impossible. But, Amat, what is it? A name or surname?

'Excuse me,' I asked the girl. 'Could you tell me what he was like, physically, I mean? The man on his own.'

The girl thought for a while.

'Sixty years old? More or less. Maybe a little older, but not much. Very white hair. Very?' She was fully concentrating, trying to recall the mysterious man's appearance. 'Well, perhaps more than white, it was grey. It's not the first time he's come. He's very thin, like he's ill or something.' She stuck up her little finger as if to illustrate the man's leanness. It was a long, ugly finger and her fingernail was too short: the girl seriously needed someone to give her a makeover. 'He always orders a bottle of red wine. Merlot, I think, and he drinks almost all of it every time. Some days he leaves something. A tip, I mean. But today, hardly anything.' Her obsession with the tip was beginning to irritate me.

I went to look for my brother to see if he could shed some light on the man. He was in a corner of the kitchen cutting up tripe for breakfast the next day and I stood there for a while admiring the way he used the knife. The food wouldn't come out half as angelic, I thought, were if not for the precision and care he puts into the preparation of every dish. To watch him clean, peel and cut vegetables, debone lamb or lightly singe the hairs on a pig's trotters is a simple pleasure that reminds me of the pure joy of the simpler things in life – things that I wish played more of a part in my life. By the time the dish has passed through the hands of a great chef and is sitting in front of you, the simple ingredients have been transformed into art. The food is, of course, delicious, but what I like best is to see him work with the raw materials, before the flame and its hallowed cooking time have transformed them.

'Yeah, a man called Amat. You don't know him. He's not from around here. He's ill. As in, he's getting towards the end. Every time he comes in, he's thinner and more yellow, or more pallid, I don't know. I'm sorry, Jordi. I'm very busy. Or do you think that I'm a writer who can spend all day doing nothing?'

My brother is an oaf, but I know that deep down he loves me. I stood blinking underneath the enormous extractor fan as he walked away into the kitchen, wiping his fingers on his apron. Amat, I asked myself. What is it? A name or a surname? So deep in thought was I that even if the kitchen assistant had dropped the broth all over the floor again, spilling it onto my shoes and burning the leather, I'm certain I wouldn't have noticed.

The next day I went to the restaurant twice. The first time was around midday, during lunch service; the second some six or seven hours later, in the evening. Amat hadn't been in; nor had he booked a table for any other day. But that wasn't the strangest part. As far as the waitress could remember under my questioning, during the days before Saint Steven's the man had once turned up without a reservation. He had booked a table for the twenty-sixth but hadn't left a telephone number or any other clue as to his identity. Amat and nothing else. Just Amat.

While not yet poisonous, my curiosity was like an intense thirst and I knew I needed to calm down. This despite my somewhat strong scepticism regarding my suspicions. The Amat that I had known some twenty years before – eighteen, to be precise – lived more than one hundred kilometres south of the city where we used to meet. The city where, ten years before, I had decided to settle down alone – rigorously alone, as I like to say – to put to rest certain things in my head and to start a new life where my younger brother, at my recommendation, had opened the restaurant which had made him famous. In addition to this, I had given up my amateur dramatics and had decided to stop trying to emulate the ill-fated Fabià Puigserver in his construction of imaginary spaces.

Thinking about it, though, the name Amat isn't that common. How many had I met over the course of my life? Him and two or three others? None of them looked anything like the description that the waitress had given me, or the age she had attributed to him. It seemed to be a good bet that it was the Amat that I had known almost twenty years before, when I was certain that theatre was my raison d'être.

I flicked through the reservation book again. Nothing shed any light on the identity of the man who would drink a whole bottle of merlot in one sitting.

'My name's Amat. As of today, I'll be your drama teacher.'

The drama room was used for music and general, after-school activities. A space of around two hundred square metres on the ground floor of my old secondary school, it was next to the room that some tragically solemn linguistic formula had decided to call The Great Hall. This Great Hall was used to give pedagogical conferences on drug addiction and adolescent sexuality. Greying people from government health departments would place folders around the room before drawing first flaccid, then erect penises on the overhead projector (cue snorts of laughter, elbows nudging left and right and groans of simulated orgasms) before moving on to internal and external female genitals (cue snorts of laughter, elbows nudging left and right and groans of simulated orgasms). To these conferences I owe my discovery of words such as 'urethra' and 'clitoris'.

On one side of the drama room was a small stage that lacked a curtain and was reached by little wooden steps. The windows on either side of the room were covered with red cellophane. On the back wall were two very narrow windows that looked like arrow slits or ventilation shafts. It was all rather dilapidated. The room's architecture was decidedly functional and the freezing cold air, from the river that ran behind the school, would slip in through the old window frames. Like the pigeon feather and bird dropping-topped asbestos-cement walls that ran around the buildings, playgrounds and car park – a patchwork of scrawls and drawings of anarchist motifs, hammers and sickles, crossed-out crosses, and erect penises entering all sorts of orifices – the drama room was the place where the clutter would end up. There was a plastic skeleton from science class, the amplifier that would make an appearance at the end of year parties, and the occasional portable heater minus the gas canister. Inside a cupboard with a door that didn't close properly were eight or nine recorders, sheet music and a tuning fork, and the ceiling was covered with cardboard eggboxes plastered with little dried spitballs.

'But Amat, what is it? A name or a surname?' asked either Anna or Selma. There weren't more than ten students in the class.

'Ah, let's not ruin the little mystery about my name just yet, ok?' he replied. 'Just call me Amat.' We tried out a few different nicknames on him, but after spending a couple of months with him, and having more than a few gin and tonics together at his house, we came to know him as just 'Amat'.

I can't imagine he was more than forty years old back then. He had started to go grey and would shave his esparto-like hair off in an attempt to control his uncontrollable curls. I couldn't have guessed what that man called Amat would awaken inside of me.

Towards the end of the seventies, people in my village still held semi-clandestine meetings in a windowless basement with part of one wall dedicated to the revolutionary bookshop, and the other three walls covered in posters that, many years later, I would have paid a small fortune for. Writers for the magazine *Horizonte*, a local publication against the dictatorship, would meet in the crypt-like basement and I occasionally accompanied my father to these meetings. Meetings, I should add, that I found incredibly long and very boring. Stuck in that smoke box for two or three hours at a time, I still don't know how my lungs weren't chronically diseased from then on. Without wishing to or realising it, my respiratory tracts absorbed smoke from the Ducados and Habanos that constantly smouldered against the fingertips of the attendees at the meeting or were propped on the edge of a Cinzano ashtray. Nobody used rolling tobacco, and the amateur revolutionary journalists would pull out their cigarettes, one after another, from the soft cigarette packets that were all the rage at the time.

Amat arrived at our secondary school towards the end of the eighties. My parents' journalist friends were by then all working for the town hall or local government and had moved away from regional Communism towards a more international Socialism that involved spending weekends away skiing and the consumption of cocaine. Back then, I had long hair that I washed just once a week, and I smoked very little: mostly marihuana, and the occasional 'normal' cigarette. I read Nietzsche's *Thus Spoke Zarathustra* and, while not understanding any of it, greatly enjoyed its solemn, sententious style. If, as many experts claim, Kafka is the greatest literary exponent of black humour, then Nietzsche is surely the philosopher of white humour. I didn't care that I couldn't understand it, it was more a case of haemorrhaging the rhetoric of my father's friends at *Horizonte*.

'There are some for whom virtue means self-flagellation,' they would shout. 'And I implore you, you have listened too much to their cries! There are others for whom virtue means falling into vice; and when their hatred and jealousy wakes up, their justice will get to work and shake open their sleepy eyes!'

A number of pages of my copy of *Thus Spoke Zarathustra* were stained with oil and if I can't tell you exactly what the book was about, I can most certainly recall the precise moment in the school canteen when said oil met said pages.

A hand came out of nowhere and gave me a friendly pat on the back. 'What are you reading?' said Amat.

Should but a simple after-school drama teacher be allowed to show such familiarity with a reader like myself, such confidence before one of his students? The man called Amat had only turned up in our class a few days before, at the start of the year and his pat made me choke on my sandwich. I was pouring over the book like a child might a new toy, soaking up old Zarathustra's curses, holding it in one hand and using the other to eat when his unfortunate pat and the brusque *deus ex machina* of newcomer's license caused me to spit a mouthful of omelette across a page of Nietzschean discourse. The food splattered against the final "Blessed be moderate poverty!" phrase and though I was able to use my nail to carefully scrape the page clean of the offending item, and I immediately ran a damp napkin across the page, an oily stain covered moderate poverty and went through to stain two more pages.

'Look what you've done,' I said rudely, without looking up.

Amat looked at me.

'I'm sorry, young man. I didn't…' As he was speaking, he turned the hand I was holding my book with so he could read the title on the front. 'But how can a boy as sensitive and intelligent as you waste your time with this ill-fated literature? Have you ever read Gombrowicz?'

'What?' I said, wondering who this idiot was to know if I was sensitive or not.

I'd never heard of the name. I assumed he was Czech. Or Polish. It was 1987, perhaps '88. My teacher opened his bag and pulled out a novel called *Pornografia*.

'Don't get too excited by the title,' he said. 'It has nothing to do with pornography. Or at least not in the, shall we say, explicit sense. You can return it when you've read it. Or, if not, you know what, it's a present. To apologise for the unfortunate omelette-spitting incident. May I sit down?'

Without waiting for a reply, he pulled back the chair in front of me and sat down.

It took me a while to dig out my copy of *Pornografia* at home. On the third page was 'Amat, August 1986' written in what appeared to be the blue ink of a cheap, dried out biro next to a small, stamp-like sticker from the Jaimes bookshop on Passeig de Gràcia. I leafed through a few of the pages. The translation, while keen, wasn't what you might call excellent. I don't know the first thing about Polish, so I ignored the hateful ellipses, the unexpected interruptions to the sentences and the passing hyphens that peppered the text. If they were fruit of the author's style or some daring new edition, then fine.

But I found it ultimately ineffective in translation.

I occasionally underlined a sentence: "It was similar to iron. To a dog lead or a recently cut tree". Regarding the story itself, I just remember that it featured two older protagonists – artists or writers – and a pair of adolescents. A girl who was engaged to a man quite a lot older than she was, if I remember correctly, and a farm boy. In one part of the novel, all four of them were walking through a forest or some field when the boy saw a worm writhing about in the middle of the path. He quickly squashed it with the pleasure and special kind of anger that only accompanies truly enjoyable actions. Even – like the worm squashing incident – when they involve certain sadistic elements. Perhaps it was simply that if the boy weren't able to break his love rival's neck, at least he could use all of his accumulated hatred and fury to crush the worm under his heel.

The phone rang as I was looking for the part about the worm. Back then, I didn't write in my books as I do now, when I jot down at the beginnings of books, the first few pages or on the covers, my impressions of standout paragraphs or mentions of what seem to me dignified ideas. I always make my notes in pencil to avoid distressing blotches and unnerving smudges from ink coming through the paper. My note making came about largely thanks to Amat's influence and his passionate way of reading. At the beginning of his classes, he would often throw some photocopies of something we weren't going to study onto our tables. A play by Joe Orton, translated by Amat himself, for example, or the first chapter of *Adolphe* by Constant, also translated by him. Even poems by Éluard or Vallejo. Amat was a representation of them all.

The phone rang and I answered. It was the restaurant and I recognised the voice of the tall waitress who had been cleaning the coffeemaker two days before. She had taken me at my word and was phoning to inform me that the lone man with his bottle of wine had just ordered dessert.

'Sara,' I said. 'Please tell him not to move. I'll be there in fifteen minutes. Make him wait, I'll pay for his drinks and his coffee. It's very important, you hear me? I have to see if it's the Amat who I think it is… I'll be there in ten, perhaps not even that.'

As I hung up, the book fell open at page eighty-five: "He wouldn't lift up his heel from the ground and the rest of the worm's body started to go rigid, moving from side to side […]. In reality there was nothing more in him than the penetration of torture, he wanted to drink it dry […] but he didn't finish the worm off […]. Henia's shoe moved forward, and she crushed the worm."

Henia was the female protagonist. I had completely forgotten.

It was a moment of exasperated eroticism, reluctantly reined in because the youngsters were restricted, or even instigated, by the contemplation of their elders. (So different, I realise now, from that piece by Bufalino in which a pair of tubercular patients are wandering through some woods close to the sanatorium where they're spending their last days. Chatting away, they mull over their scant expectations of life and the younger one ends up crushing a worm and setting it on fire. Nobody else sees the agonising spectacle and death). Rereading the Pole's lines as I was about to leave, I was overwhelmed by aromas of a field brimming with flowers and herbs, the rustic smell of mud, the scent of the two protagonists' warm skin, perhaps even the stench of a mangy dog. Though perhaps I am confusing sensations and people; it is something I often do. But I mostly thought back to the time when I had first read the book and many others like it and the circumstances that had made it possible. I put on my anorak and went out into the street.

I got to the restaurant in less than fifteen minutes. Once the client had been alerted by the waitress about what was going on, it seems that he had become somewhat uncomfortable as if he were suddenly in a great hurry and didn't want to meet a stranger. Perhaps he felt ill at ease with the possibility of the person in question turning out to be someone important from his past. He must have joined the dots: the chef had the same name as a young man who had made up part of his circle of friends many years ago. My surname isn't a very common one, especially in the centre of the country: in the north one can find a number of us, but not here. Well, the man had left without waiting for me. He must have been afraid of something. What could possibly have gone through the head of that gaunt, old man, prematurely aged by the hypothetical illness attributed to him by my brother?

'He's yellow,' my brother confirmed. 'And even thinner than before.'

It seemed my suspicions were getting closer to their resolution: if he left, it's probably him. If not, why would the man leave when told that someone wanted to say hello and, what's more, pay for his coffee and drinks?

'Sara! For goodness' sake!' I shouted, frustrated at the situation. 'Why didn't you keep him here?'

She told me that he hadn't eaten very much, just one course of veal – I don't remember the side – and had only touched one piece of bread. The girl added that this time he had only asked for a glass, and not a whole bottle. There was a violet shadow in his glass. A good detective, I thought, would start there; with the fingerprints on the stem and the stain of his lips on the leading edge of the bowl.

He had also chosen a dessert (an unfinished chocolate coulant) and had had a coffee.

'He left this,' said the waitress bad-temperedly, and she threw something across the table where the enigmatic diner had been sitting and that I was now examining to try and make out some clue to his identity from between the breadcrumbs and the sediment of the wine sitting in the bottom of his glass. 'Your brother says that you should give it back to him, as you're the one who knows him. By the way, he looked a lot worse, your friend,' she added, ironically underlining the expression. 'But at least today he left a tip!'

The girl's tone was offhand, if not rather unpleasant. The tone of someone shaking off a worrying subject. I found that her obsession with the tip lowered the establishment's elegant pretensions of sophistication, as if it were one of those cheap bar restaurants with torn paper tablecloths, half-dissolved and crinkled by fizzy water, leaving but the plastic table cover and thick wine glasses with cigarette butts afloat on the last dregs.

It was a well-worn red plastic wallet. The kind of thing you might keep your driving license or credit cards in; a kind of folder that opened up like a book. Of the two transparent sheets of plastic inside marking the two sections, one was about to come unstuck and the other, slightly more intact one, was sticky to the touch as if it had been covered for a long time by a sticker that had just come off. Or perhaps it was the rest of the wallet's grimy cover that gave it its horrible sticky quality.

The waitress went off to the kitchen and I told myself that it was all just one big joke, a random whim, and I threw the wallet to one side like someone dumping a playing card. It was then that I noticed the remains of some letters, golden in colour and almost faded away, on one of sides of the case: U OES OL O SIN OL. Nothing else remained. Just below the half-disappeared inscription I recognised a faint picture of an old-fashioned car with its enormous exterior horn and oversized rear wheels. It was enough for me to know that it was the Amat I was looking for, and that he had left the relic so that I might recognise him. Confound him, I thought. You won't get away that easily!

Memory doesn't require much: the vestiges of some letters cut into a worn tombstone and gnawed away by erosion; the half-erased name and some illegible, neglected dates. Just as a tombstone marks someone's whole life, regardless of how miserable it has been, so I had this: a simple, well-worn wallet of broken red plastic like the ones people used to keep their driving license in, fitting into the back pocket of your jeans like a glove. The kind that, with the rush of life and the rub of your fingers and trousers, ends up losing the inscription that once adorned one of its faces and the drawing of the logo, now long out of fashion. No need for anything else: from here, anyone unravelling the thread of memory will continue until the whole reel has come undone. Then, cut free from the yarn where it was sleeping, the man, or perhaps the embalmed corpse of the man we are searching for, will appear to us. When we start to dig up our memories, above all when we bring back to the present remote passages from our lives, it means untangling different figures from the past. It's like setting the nativity scene. We take some characters, the gestures and gaits – or perhaps the unabashed behaviour – of misrepresented people. And despite all this, once we have placed the shepherd under the lights and the fisherman is sitting solemnly next to his silver river, crossed a few metres further down by a little bridge, the line from his rod appearing to sink down into it, and the mountains of cork or bark have been topped with freshly-picked moss, once the sand is gold like the desert, the chickens are pecking at crumbs on the path, and the roof over the doorway is covered in snow; only then do our hearts light up in recognition of the scene. The figures, at least in our eyes, are still the same age, and everything is as it has always been.

And so, back to the embalmed corpse of the man. Let's unwrap the bandages, retrieve his physique, resurrect his eyes – dead to our memories – and take up once again the thread of our tale.

Amat's eyes weren't any bigger or more beautiful than other eyes but they were more enchanting than any I have ever had the pleasure or the panic of staring into, regardless of gender. It upset me to think that time and illness, if my brother was right, had clouded over his inquisitive, unnerving intensity.

Staring at each of us, first one, then another, he wore a high-necked grey jumper with a white badge with the words 'Way to blue' on it, though I didn't realise until around fifteen years later that it was the name of a song. He would hold a lit cigarette between his forefinger and thumb as if hiding it, causing the smoke to billow out from within the bowl of his hand like a soul trying to escape from a skull. Sitting around his melamine table in the flat on Carrer dels Grecs, that he shared with a couple of bearded Argentines who looked like devout followers of Cortázar or Daniel Viglietti, we would look at him as he stubbed them out only half smoked while he told us something important. There were a great number of books standing on the floor that supported the others that sat above them. We never went into his bedroom: it was the only part of the flat that was off limits and the way he spoke about it kept it shrouded in mystery. A mystery that was reinforced by the legend of the small laminated sign he himself had designed that said: 'The Final Resting Place of Amat'. When he wanted, he could be very truculent. It never occurred to any of us to go anywhere near the door handle to open it, to disturb the peace within, be it a raging inferno, an unmade bed, or a caged monkey.

'This poem you've written about skin blemishes has some good ideas,' he said to me one day, 'but your execution is terrible.'

The half-smoked cigarette flew off the balcony and down to the street below with me trying to digest or spit out his words. The word, in fact. Everything he said influenced us too much, whether it was a reprimand or measured eulogy, a piece of advice or an act of censorship. Only two or three months had passed since he had started to give drama classes for our group, and there was already a closeness between us more like cousins than what you might expect from a relationship between a teacher and his students in the first term of the year. He had taught us to truly read! And I accompany the sentence with an exclamation mark because, if I look back at my life, nobody has ever shown me the secrets of reading in the same depth as he did. Right then, however, I just didn't want to believe that my mentor had called my poem 'terrible'. Especially as I was only just starting to sketch out my first few poems and to measure the beauty of the world with the rough wooden spoon of my incipient and, most probably, indefensible texts. And perhaps its horrors, too. During adolescence, one is oversensitive to the injustices and the rawest expressions of barbarity, with one's weak, eager words as defence. As such, on that day I felt the urge to follow the curve of light from the cigarette as it made its way out into the night air. Carrer dels Grecs is one of the wildest streets in the town and opposite Amat's flat was an empty piece of land with a metal gate that would growl like an animal in the wind. A colony of cats lived there, and I watched the red light of the cigarette go out before rows of feline eyes, lit up in the dark. Not five hundred metres separated Amat's flat and the revolutionary crypt where my father had once conspired. Ten years had passed. An eternity.

One midday I asked him for the keys to his flat. I knew that in the afternoon I had to go into the city to pick up some books that had arrived for me from France. It was the day that my relationship with Selma started. And it started right there within the four walls where Amat lived. During the first few weeks it was wonderful, but a little before Easter it had become so poisonous that it all ended in flames. We spent two hours on that uncomfortable sofa. I can't now remember what, but I know we drank something and smoked a little, too. Afterwards she put on her knickers, exhibiting a certain discreet elegance when lifting one leg first, and then the other. I don't think I've ever mentioned Selma before. When she was sixteen years old, she had undergone a heart operation and I found the subsequent scar on her breast very sexy. She would joke that her flat chest was the result of the doctors opening up her heart and placing a zip across it.

'Flesh that doesn't pad out the bones,' she would say, 'that doesn't cling to the skeleton, that most flaccid of flesh, is always looking for a way out.'

Her knickers were white and when she went to the toilet, I heard the powerful, equine sound of the stream against the bowl and the pull of the toilet chain. I assumed she was still cleaning up or sorting out her hair, and it never occurred to me that perhaps I too should go and clean up. Goodness knows what she must have thought. Instead, I took advantage of the couple of free minutes to take a peek inside our teacher's bedroom. It was a case of the idea coming into my head and doing it without thinking and what I saw within Amat's resting place – his body yet absent – confirmed my suspicions that he really was a very strange person indeed. It saddened me to know that I would never completely understand him. As such, I wanted to even more. The discovery made my heart sink, because up until that day I had never admired anyone so much. Was I disappointed? Did I consider seeing that an aberration? What could that absurd scene mean? The little lit bedside lamp, the multi-coloured flag, all those off-putting but ever so slightly irresistible images hanging off the walls. And what did the layout of the room mean? The bed, the two chairs, all those pairs of trousers, the mountain of shoes. I should never have pushed open the door, carried away by my own unhealthy curiosity!

'My door is always open to you,' he would say, in a matter of fact way. 'Or almost always open; as long as nothing comes up which might require a certain amount of intimacy. Everything except this door.' He walked up to the door and knocked on it hard as if announcing a visitor. 'Not here. Ever. Abandon hope, all ye who enter.'

He stared at us again. His eyes could hurt you. And he would utter words, sometimes whole verses, that we could only vaguely follow at the best of times, ever quoting from the very highest of highbrow books. We were young and naïve and were rehearsing *The Bald Soprano* by Ionesco that we were going to perform at the end of the course. I had been given the role of Mr. Smith, and Selma was my wife. She wore one of her grandmother's gowns that smelt terribly of mothballs. Years later, reminiscing on my own particular representation of the character, I realised that we weren't ready to understand a great amount of what Amat would say to us during our friendship. I would be reading a book and suddenly find something I felt I'd heard before. Another day, when studying an author or reading a poet, I would come up against words that would seduce me in a way that was both strange and powerful. Quite apart from the beauty of the poetry, the verse had stuck in my memory from so many years before, and there was always a faint memory there of

Amat. Reading those verses was to bring our friend back from the dead. From our loss of contact.

I went into his bedroom. I was unable to undo what had brought me to extend my nervous hand to the door handle and to cast my scholarly eye around the heart of the shadows of his final resting place.

And now, because of my transgression, I would have to live with a terrible secret.

'All of this is yours,' he had said, trusting us completely, 'right and left, but you must not eat the forbidden fruit from this tree.'

I couldn't tell my friends. And I most definitely couldn't tell Amat. I had let myself down, and he would never forgive me. The problem now was all of my own making: I would have to pretend as if I hadn't seen anything. To play dumb. To turn a blind eye.

'What's up with you?' asked Selma. 'You're as white as a sheet. Didn't you like it?'

I had closed the door before she came out of the bathroom. If someone had stabbed me there and then, I'm certain that not a drop of blood would have come out of me.

'Did I like it? I liked it too much! Come here, I'll tuck the label in.'

It was the fourth or fifth time that I had been with a girl. The other times had been with Amèlia, a second cousin of mine with a great body and who was great in bed, but who had started to get obsessive, laughing like a crazy person after sex.

I couldn't get what I had seen in Amat's room out of my head, but just a few weeks later I went back there one evening, this time with him. Back to terra incognita.

It was the saddest, most boring Christmas of my life. I couldn't celebrate it with anyone. At the end of summer, I had broken up with a girl. We had gone to Crete together and our conflict began on the beach at Matala. There are deep caves there, cut out of the cliffs, the fruit of a thousand of years of erosion, and the Romans had used them to build a cemetery. A group of hippies had moved into them in the sixties. We climbed up to one of these caves having spent the whole morning arguing. It was like a prison cell. The sandy floor was scattered with rubbish and the walls were covered with English words scratched into the crumbling walls. She was carrying a bottle of water in her hand and, on her back, she had a bag with the six most important things when travelling around an island: identity documents, a guidebook, car keys, a purse, tampons, and mints. I was refusing to agree with her about something that I no longer remember, and she got angry and pushed me. There and then we both decided that each of us would continue the holiday alone. I left her the car keys and went off to find another car rental place. There were only three days left of the trip, and I spent them shut up in a hotel room next to the shipyards in the city of Canea. As of August, we had spoken only three or four times.

An old friend called me on the first of January. He asked me to go that same afternoon to a hospital in Barcelona, while warning me that it was a delicate situation. When I got to the hospital, I was shocked to see Muntsa Arnau, a girl who had been in the same year as me at secondary school. In the end-of-year performance – the risky Ionesco play that I mention above – she hadn't had a specific role as such, but played some pieces on the violin. The video from that June performance in 1988 showed her walking across the stage in the dark, dressed all in white. The stage light followed her as she walked very slowly, playing her piece, her pale white skin and black eyeliner making her look almost spectral. Outside her room, the friend who had called me (and who, unlike me, had stayed in contact with her) told me that she would recognise me but wouldn't be able to talk.

'She's very ill. It's now just a matter of time.'

I approached the bed and was confronted by a vaguely recognisable shadow from my past. I touched the upturn of the quilt, and she put her hand on mine. It wasn't really a stroke, but at least she recognised me and, in a performance of smiles that she must have practised dozens of times in the preceding few days, she said goodbye to me. Her hand was cold and so repulsive to touch that it brought out goose bumps on my skin. I relived an age-old memory: I had once fallen asleep in a wood and an abandoned dog had woken me up with its slobbering by drooling on my face. Perhaps what I really disliked about poor ill-stricken Muntsa's hand was that I could imagine it already touching the door on the other side.

My friend and I and a man I didn't know sought refuge for a few minutes in the hospital café. Looking at each other in silence, we raised our eyebrows and shrugged our shoulders and I emptied the sachet of sugar that had come with my coffee onto the green lacquer table. Using the stirring implement, a kind of transparent, plastic pole, I formed it into three or four lines as if it were a strange sort of unrefined cocaine. Our generation had started to die, and we had nothing better to do than to pour sugar onto the table, shrug our shoulders and scratch the backs of our necks. To say nothing, and make it no more explicit than it already was. The girl at the till wore a red hat with a white bobble and to her right was a display of crisps and snacks. Just below her was a box full of packets of chewing gum, liquorice and coffee-flavoured sweets. From my chair, I saw the fridge where they kept the blue bottles of mineral water and fruit salads.

'This is Pere,' my friend said, introducing me to the other man. 'Muntsa's husband. You've been married for what, ten years?' The man nodded his head, adding 'and a half.'

'They have two beautiful children.'

I reached over and held his hand.

'I'm sorry, Pere. It must be terrible.'

Pere's mobile started ringing and my friend and I went back to being silent. He put his hand in front of his mouth, but we could hear what the poor man was saying, his answers to the questions on the other end of the line. I played with the scattered sugar.

'I don't think so, no… not much, well… We're also hoping that… yes, at some time.' He started to sob. 'Thank you… we're not going anywhere… Don't worry, my sister is looking after them… Yes. Thanks. No, no. Ok… Goodbye. Thank you.'

He hung up the phone and apologised. My friend and I looked at each other. There was nothing else to say. Pere went back to the room. Halfway down the hallway, an elderly couple stopped him. The woman hugged him tight and burst into tears and the man placed his hand on his shoulder. They could have been Pere's parents, or perhaps his parents-in-law.

'You know who I'm going to see,' I said to my friend, 'one of these days?'

'No idea,' he replied comforted, perhaps, that we had finally been able to break the silence. It was now just the two of us, without the burden of pain beating next to us. In moments like those, one can only accompany: to share is little less than impossible.

'I'll give you a clue: a teacher from secondary school who… who made an impression.'

He all of a sudden seemed more interested in my riddle.

'Mrs. Clavero from Spanish lit.?'

'A male teacher,' I said. 'We only had him for a year. An after-school class…'

'Get out of here: Amat? The drama guy? You're still trying to get in touch with him? Where have you found him?'

'We haven't seen each other yet. But it won't be long before we do…'

We had to interrupt the conversation because Selma appeared in the café. She hugged my friend and started to cry. She had put on a lot of weight. She said hello to me and gave me a kiss on my cheek before sitting down with us.

'So, what now?' she asked.

'It is what it is,' said my friend. 'It's bad. Very bad. A question of hours, perhaps.'

Muntse didn't die until the thirteenth of January.

I didn't hear anything else from Amat. On the night of the Kings' celebration, I saved myself the sight of the black king's grotesque, boot-polished face and escaped from the noise in the squares and avenues, saving myself from the hailstorm of sweets that were slung out over the crowds by people on the floats and avoiding parents carrying their children on their shoulders. I was once told that the blacked-up kings would sweat so much that the thick, dark paint on their cheeks would drip down and stain the carmine of their lips. Many of the Christmas decorations had taken on a pathetic, incorrigibly sad aspect, like torn primary school posters in the last days of June. Of the street bulbs shaped like stars or reindeers, a few were still lit up, but the majority were either broken or dark. I find that the end of the festive period is when one is most convinced of the complete futility of life. That which twenty days earlier looked like a magnificent fruit, ripe for the picking, is now nothing but hogwash that you don't know what to do with. It's the sensation that time, more than in any other part of the year, has completely and utterly disappeared. It also happens in summer, from the Sant Joan celebrations to the end of August, but we have the comfort of many more days to get used to the idea. One less Christmas in our lives followed by reserved Christmas tree spaces in the rubbish: leave yours here…

I got to my brother's restaurant and was presented with a bowl of stewed chickpeas, bacon fat and shitake mushrooms, all seasoned with chives. I sat at a window table and ate it slowly, honouring the chef with a sports newspaper open to one side, savouring every mouthful. It was starting to rain outside and some of the children still perched on their parents' shoulders started to squirm nervously, intransigently tugging on their mother's or father's hair and urging them back home faster. I heard the ringing of a distant phone and the order from a head waiter back to the kitchen. A fork fell onto the floor and the waitress replaced it with a new one. A woman of around thirty, wearing a dress that was too thin for the time of year and a necklace of green stones, was laughing loudly. My brother was speaking on the phone and he beckoned me over, gesturing me to pick up the other phone in the office. Picking it up to listen in, I arrived at the end of the brief conversation. The voice was that of an old man with breathing problems. Though I hadn't heard the voice for a long time, I recognised it immediately, retrieving the familiarity of the tone and rhythm like actors do when clearly pronouncing things. So many years later, there it was, the same voice that spoke to us, class in, class out, at breaktimes in the corridor-thin Beckenbauer bar, set between the Edelweiss dry cleaner's, that in our second year became a pre-prepared food place called Al Punt de Sal, and the Rossinyol driving school. A single table for lunch was booked for the tenth, a Saturday. Finally, we would meet.

Two months later, I received an anonymous letter. On the postmark was the name of a Spanish village called El Pedernoso and, looking it up on the internet, I saw it was in Cuenca. What was he doing in Cuenca?

He first apologised for his 'strange behaviour' in the restaurant. He had, he wrote, known that the establishment belonged to my brother and, while he didn't consider himself to be a man of great taste, he liked the finer things in life and here he provided a number of gastronomic observations and wrote at length about some of his favourite wines, none of which I had heard of. He also mentioned that he considered the best dish in the restaurant to be the suckling pig, something that had been confirmed by a fine review that my little brother's restaurant, and that dish in particular, had received from a newspaper supplement not long after the festive period. The letter was handwritten and all of this introduction, which I skimmed over quickly, served only to make me even more nervous.

Why was he writing me a letter? Nobody sends letters these days. And why did he not put a sender's address? Throughout the summer after our school year together, we had written back and forth to each other. Back then, though, before email, between one card and the other there was always a break of five or six days, and if we were waiting for an answer to a question in one of our letters, well then you'd have to wait five or six days more. Over the two months of holidays, you might expect to receive some ten letters and this meant that, in each of them, you had to include the week's essential news, comments on books you were reading and information on the places and cities that you had visited.

In the second paragraph he wrote that he had heard about Muntsa Arnau's death and expressed his condolences. He didn't say who had told him, but it suddenly occurred to me that over all these years someone had secretly been in touch with him. Perhaps the same person who gave him my address. The informant, however, had fulfilled his or her duties a little too late and Amat had only found out about her death on the day of her funeral, by which time it was far too late for him to make it. Though even if he had known, I doubt he would have attended. The question about whether I was in touch with him or not, that my friend asked me while we were waiting in the cafeteria for poor Muntse to die, came to mind.

He also explained that it had been he who had sent the ribbon-less wreath of red carnations that had been laid at the foot of the coffin. At the end of our Ionesco performance, he had given Muntse a bouquet of the same flowers.

It was from the third paragraph that I started to understand a great many things and was able to answer some of the questions that had hung obsessively over me for two or three years after first meeting him. The answers, however, came late, far too late. He assured me that he would have been happy to meet me face to face and that, as such, he had phoned the restaurant and had booked a table for the tenth of January. That was a little more than two months ago: I was reading the letter on the day before Saint Joseph's. He had the feeling that I would be informed immediately. Some days before he had left a token on the table to be recognised by, a token that he still kept from back when the workers at the driving school would look for potential customers in the students who occupied the tables in the Beckenbauer, giving them keyrings, pens and wallets. The same token, like a glove bearing all of the hallmarks of the person to whom it belongs, that I had picked up.

'You betrayed yourself that day. I knew immediately that you had entered my bedroom, that you'd taken a peek. Why did you do it? Don't you remember that I didn't speak to you for a few days afterwards?'

He had attached proof of my treachery to the letter: a tiny, thin piece of paper, the crumpled shard of a train ticket that, returning to the living room in the fear that Selma had already left the bathroom and, horrified, had seen my betrayal, had fallen out of my pocket and had never since crossed my mind. To have in my hands that insignificant slip of paper was a broadside from the past, like a photograph of an old friend from twenty years earlier. Amat, that wily fox, knew it had to be mine because the girl who had followed me to his flat didn't use the train.

Despite all this, he explained, he had decided to forgive me.

'Back then, I was thirty-seven years old and you were all sixteen or seventeen. But of all my students, you were my favourite.'

My heart jumped. His favourite. Back in those days, our group was so small that I would never in my life have considered myself to be the "favourite," but I have to confess that I felt flattered by the statement. A few weeks after the incident in Amat's flat with Selma, he invited me to dinner and I gladly accepted as I was worried that our drama teacher had been more distant that usual. During the meal, we spoke about books and the play we were rehearsing. We also spoke about the girls in our group, and it seemed as if he had forgotten his suspicious coldness of the weeks before. Amat was one of us, something that provoked mistrust in some of the other teachers who did not look kindly on another member of staff being so intimate with the students, being just one more member of the group. Of the conversation that I remember that evening, we were a little bawdy when speaking about Helena and Selma and I laughed a lot. He asked me if I had had fun with Selma, that day on the sofa, and he winked at me on the sly. Finished up, I accompanied him back to Carrer dels Grecs and he invited me up to his flat for 'one for the road'.

We drank our drinks together before I accompanied my professor into his room, acting as if it were the first time I had crossed the threshold into his 'final resting place', though of course it wasn't. It was nothing like the unnerving place that I had glimpsed a few weeks before and I felt honoured by his attention.

In the last paragraph, he explained why he had disappeared in the summer of '88. He bid me a brusque farewell and told me not to try and find him. He was ill and his spirit needed peace. Finishing his letter with a simple 'Goodbye', his last words were defiant as ever:

'One of these days, someone will inform you that I am dead. That is my destiny.'

THE LINDEN TREE

Dear reader, now that the book you have in your hands is coming to an end and a mere few pages separate you from the words 'The End', I wanted not only to use them to indicate the end of the book, but also to represent the passing of the moment and, at the same time, the birth of a new period in what I hope will be your long and fertile life. And so perhaps now is a good moment to tell you a real love story. In a marked difference from the other stories you have read here, there will be no ghosts, no deranged women. There will be no ethereal spectres springing open the bolts to the catacombs of former days, to cousins back from nothingness or to corpses in various states which, for many moons now, have slept soundly in the cemetery of our consciousness and which, after a while, memory desires to dig up: a bow-thin tibia; a rosary made up of the bones from a foot; scraps of burial shrouds. This time we have a flesh and blood protagonist, a woman who is the sole object of the love of which I now write. You will find no shadow of anxiety and no motive for anguish or pain, though a certain melancholy is spread throughout the story as if a love story could be written any other way. There are wines that, so as to appreciate their value, need to be decanted before drinking: in this case, our melancholy will serve as the decanter to this story. I hope, dear reader, that that which I am about to tell you will comfort you with an intimate, rather than intense, pleasure, a secret pleasure if you will. And until the moment you start to lose your senses, like the wine from the superior vintage that, once tasted, is of such excellence that we are unable to stop drinking until the whole bottle has been consumed. Our judgement, perhaps, is not yet clouded, though it is not far off. For me, right now, it is as if I am the proud owner of a wine that has spent countless years resting in a glass bottle. Imagine it: wrap it in cobwebs and encrust it in the cold dust of your cellar. And so I pour this wine, this metaphor for my story, down to the last drop into a cut-glass decanter. It has not yet settled and tiny bubbles run like pearls around the edge of the liquid, now defined by the outline of the glass: natural evolution, much more sophisticated than the kraters used by the Greeks and Romans in which those ancient civilisations would mix the divine fermented grape juice with pure water – the clay of the krater, at times decorated with tiny figures, with friezes, hid the natural colour of the poor wine it held. If I stir the liquid a little, the tears dance down the glass leaving their fiery shadows across the transparent body, a shadow made up of ephemeral candles. The liquid is black and violet, at times red under the light. I need but one glass, nothing more. Be kind enough to bring it over to me. It'll be worth it, you'll see. The wine is served, as is my story, and I trust, dear, patient reader, it will not disappoint.

Can one love an older woman? Meeting her in the last season of her life, some seven decades under her belt, when the wrinkles on her face confirm the tightening and wringing out of her skin through all of its functions, far from the creams and remedies, from the massages, disaccustomed of caresses and strokes, now beneath the sun's raw rays, now under rain, at other times buffeted by a gust of hailstones. Can one love someone who, as we say around here, is already made, with beautiful blue eyes, two drops of eternal colour that will never fade or dwindle until her body is encased in wood, and the hair that I myself have seen turn from grey to the same white colour as the poplar flowers, like dried foam, that coat the edges of the path up to her house every May, like snow out of season? Someone whose smile disarms or cheers you up just by the sight of it? Someone who, perhaps without realising it, possesses the strange beauty of a smile made with dull, aged lips, without lipstick, cut by the cold of time, set like a belt around the false teeth that occasionally dance around her mouth; a smile so faithful to her kind soul that it represents her like a face in a painting? I say you can. Of course you can love the person I have started to describe, the person you will soon get to know a lot better. Not unlike your wife or your very own children, the links with whom are, of course, much stronger, more lasting; but also like the ties that are more exposed to the scissors of betrayal, those that never escape the feeling of possession that govern our love for them. Or the woodworm of jealousy. But what law of possession can poison the relationship that we have with our grandmother-in-law, an adopted grandmother who continues even when, of the four blood grandparents only one remains and who, despite all this, has never once wanted to fulfil their role? A woman who, when this story starts in the paragraph below, is seventy-two years old and, when it finishes a few pages later, is eighty-eight? A grandmother as dear to you as any friend. The proud owner of a personality and blessed elegance on which no burden weighs, before whom you feel no need to show your merits or to prove anything because the understanding you have with the elderly woman has been, from the very first moment, complete. The story, dear reader, you hold now in your hands aims to express this deep love.

I had fallen in love with her granddaughter, a girl just eighteen years old. Back then I was still young, though I was twenty-five, an age at which the writer Hermann Hesse – so well received by new readers and hopeless idealists – considered himself to be passed his youth only nine decades before. I met the subject of the story one Sunday in November in a local market in a town close to my own. My young love couldn't drive yet and so had been accompanied by her grand-mother who drove an old van that, had you not seen it being driven but rather parked up in some corner of the world, you would have concluded it to have been waiting to be turned into scrap metal. Tiny as it was, you would hardly be able to make out the grey fringe sitting behind the enormous steering wheel. I had no doubt seen the van as I went about my business for many years before meeting her granddaughter. Living out of town, she would drive into the centre to buy a few fillets of meat from the butcher or pick up her post and a newspaper from the post office. This, while I would have been on the pavement on my way to pick up the kids from school or going to the swimming pool in summer to bathe there uncomfortably, surrounded by women shouting and smoking, and their badly behaved children who would throw each other's goggles into the water or roll up their towels and whip them across the thighs of others, producing instantaneous howls.

When fate brought us together on the same road, I would beep the horn and lift my hand from the steering wheel to say hello. But she never saw me, concentrating rather on her driving or on the flowers that shoot up in spring and summer and which bring colour to the thick grass in the ditches, as if they were the last shoots that had seen life below the ground in the silent current of the recent rain-water and the infinite subterranean processes. Getting back home, it would not be out of the ordinary for her to be carrying a bouquet of flowering nettles, of yellow wild mustard, of bright orange marigold, or petite forget-me-nots with their five perfect blue petals that are so easily pressed between the pages of a book. I doubt there is even one flower in the whole country that, over her long years of life, she had not considered, first with her vivid eyes and, after, with her busy fingers. She would get home and take an old vase out of some wardrobe and half fill it with water from the tap. She would then place the handful of wildflowers into it and combine the colours – the broken blue and white of her eyes at the front; the green of the asparagus on top; behind, the yellow that she so loved; and here and there, joyous blue – to produce, sensitive reader, a bridal bouquet more delicate than any to have ever come from an Amsterdam florist. At times, however, the beauty of the colours would come second in priority to the sensations of their aromas: torn samples of thyme, rosemary or lavender that she would leave to dry on her bedside table, waterless and free of vase or dented can, next to an alarm clock that was always either a few minutes fast or slow. But that didn't matter because she would get up when her heart chose to raise her from her bed - generally at around six in the morning.

Many years have passed since that first Sunday when we met, when I would follow in the footsteps of the girl I had fallen for. Yet I remember it well. The vibrant, colourful market was in full swing along a wide open area at the entrance to the village. The village wasn't entirely ugly, but it had grown too fast and the chaotic planning had ruined its appearance. The village I remembered from an old black-and-white postcard from the sixties showed open vineyards and, in the distance, a clutch of houses set around a bell tower that

had escaped the ravages of war. There must have been some celebration because on the same open ground I mentioned, long before
reaching the stalls selling clothes and leather goods, cheeses, honey,
salt cod and meats, there was a circus tent with discoloured pink
and blue triangles along its edges. Here and there, I saw strange
looking animals with sad, withered faces. I recognised a vicuña, a
dromedary and a camel that were grazing, or at least trying to graze,
in a spot covered by dried grasses. Two goats were tethered to the
struts that supported the sign saying Cirque de Paris at the ends of
long ropes. Also, chickens with dark plumage, as if imported from a
remote latitude or time, and seven or eight dogs with coats picked at
by various parasites. They were dogs free of any signs of breed: you
might say they were street dogs, if the streets in question included
the different filthy paths, suburban wastelands and hills from which
all rock or chalk has long since been extracted and which are now
used as tips where tonnes and tonnes of rubbish now ferment in
the summer heat. In the shade of the canvas, locked in a rusty cage,
there might have been a sleeping, diseased tiger or a toothless lion. I
remember thinking it strange that the police hadn't yet intervened in
that group of beasts from Paris, that hospice of the dead and dying,
and that they hadn't clapped its owners in irons.

I parked close to the watchful, worn animals and there was
a moment when, walking through some fields on my way to the
market, the vicuña stared at me with an excruciating sadness as if
it were begging me: 'Free me from this hell, happy passer-by. Kill
my owner with a dagger or cave his head in with a broken stone,
brave young man. Take me away to Scandinavia or Siberia or to Rio
de Janeiro, if you want, to pull on even the heaviest carnival floats,
the ones most bursting with unctuous flesh. Nothing can be worse
than this.'

I hurried past and got to the market, where the unavoidable cries of gypsies were advertising offers for underwear at one hundred cents, skirts for two euros fifty, and three pairs of socks for eighty cents. The girl and her grandmother were already there, and I walked up behind the girl in silence before covering her eyes and asking her: 'Who is it?'

The grandmother's smile said it all: 'Hello. Finally we can put a face to the voice from all those telephone calls!'

I gave her a kiss on each cheek, following the protocol that I imagined I had to, but she told me that she didn't like greeting people with kisses. She said that people who give kisses out to all and sundry inspired little confidence in her. Her skin was dry, cracked here and there by wrinkles. Her eyes, so very blue, were smiling like two cartoon caricatures with lives of their own. Years later, after her illness and during my saddest days with her, I decided never to refuse kisses to my children, her great grandchildren. She would stroke the hair that hung down my elder child's forehead while assuring him, time and again – her memory going as she started repeating things – that his hair was the spitting image of her mother's; hair that would never be subdued by a comb or parting, hair that human hands found impossible to dominate. The boy had dark skin too, like his great-great grandmother. I had always imagined that cowlick on the old woman's forehead as they were carrying her off to be buried. Seeing it through the glass of the coffin; a characteristic stamp of her appearance, a rebel quiff in the blazing fringe of life! And I found it incredible that a century later, through long rivers of blood, a similar cowlick, a marker of one's appearance, should find itself resuscitated on my own son's forehead. Though for my little girl, her great-grandmother's attention would fall on her teeth.

'How well set,' she'd say. 'And how very white!' Though they were already turning a little yellow.

I have often maintained that the first time you see someone you can already tell a lot about their personality. While somebody else's eyes might judge or hide from you, that old lady greeted me with a wink that might or might not have actually happened, but that I remember all the same. That Sunday market, in a November now many years ago, I was unable to imagine how the woman I had just met was to influence my life to such a degree that, year after year, I found I was asking myself more and more what she would do or how she would deal with certain problems. I still ask myself these things today, so many years later. This despite the fact that her illness impaired her reasoning, even if it is but her memory. The pain, however, wasn't able to dim her gaze.

That morning, she asked me how my classes were going because her granddaughter had told her that I was working as a professor of languages. I answered vaguely, and she confessed that, had it not been for the war, she too would have liked to have been a teacher.

'Though teacher and professor aren't the same,' she said. 'despite my lack of studies, this much I know. I would have liked to have taught children to read and write. And a few numbers to see them straight through life.'

The girl had gone on ahead and was now looking over a pile of unlabelled jumpers at a market stall. She moved the pile to one side before picking out a few more. There were mountains of them: some without a bag, some lacking a hanger, others that had been abandoned or were different sizes or colours.

'What do you think of this one,' the girl asked her grandmother.

It was a baggy red woollen jumper. In those days she never wore fitted shirts or t-shirts that might cling to her figure, but rather loose-fitting jumpers, ones that tend to stretch and get worn away by leaving little pills of wool all around the house. It was the first piece of clothing I remember from our relationship. A few winters later, by then dull and worn, the jumper was still able to conjure up memories as I folded it up amongst the other items of clothing I had just taken off the clothesline and that didn't need ironing.

'I'm not sure I should be the one to answer this kind of question,' replied the grandmother. 'Now that you have a much more reliable advisor.'

That year, the girl appeared in that red jumper in a multitude of photos. I pretended to pay attention to the quality of the wool, touching the sleeves and the neck, even rubbing it up against my freshly shaved cheeks.

'I think I'd find it itchy. I'm very fussy about wool. I just can't…'

Giving her back the jumper, I link my fingers with hers.

The jumper no longer itched. The wool was now a marvel of smoothness and smelled wonderful: no damp or dusty market aromas, nothing but mint and fennel.

'You know, there's a poem, I can't remember who it's by, but it'll come to me, about just this: two boys are secretly holding hands in a shop. One minds the shop and the other one makes out that he's a customer. I think they're talking about handkerchiefs, but I'm not sure.

My desire was burning hotter than the November sun, veiled by wispy clouds. I thought about it, and said nothing. But it was as if I had. My loved one looked at me in the way she once did when we would touch each other. She had green eyes that would turn a light reddish brown, like the colour of tea, depending on the light. They weren't blue like her grandmother's who, with discreet wisdom, had gone on a few steps ahead and was now pretending to be looking at some embroidered handtowels that were hanging from some thread.

That was the first time. And I was conscious of having met a person touched by light.

At the stall with the pots and pans we bought a simple, practical example in which, the next winter, before we went to live at the grandmother's house but when we were already spending almost every weekend there, I would heat up the milk for breakfast on Sunday mornings while the girl was still asleep in bed and her grandmother had already gone out to look for herbs on the pathways around her house.

'What are you writing?' asks the woman as she walks over to him and touches his hair while he sits in front of his computer. She is carrying a steaming mug in her hand the contents of which won't go cold for a few minutes more. She can't sleep unless she has had a mug of herbal tea. Even if it has gone cold.

'Nothing, the story that I told you yesterday, a… a tribute, a homage? I suppose you could call it that. And I suppose that, of everything that I've written, it's been the most difficult. But also the most necessary.

'May I?' she asks as she takes a look at the screen. The days are stifling. The air conditioning is on. The machine is plugged in and a red light is showing. This summer the fearful tiger mosquito has started to run riot across the skins of the locals.

If he should now lift up his head, he would see his wife reading not in total silence and moving her lips: "You know, there's a poem, I can't remember who it's by, but it'll come to me, about just this: two boys are secretly holding hands in a shop. One minds the shop and the other one makes out that he's a customer."

"I can't remember?"

'Well, let's call it… prosaic licence.

'I suppose so. And can you remember the poem in question now?'

'Of course I can. Look...'

The man gets up and walks over to a shelf on the wall opposite where he writes and picks out a green book. She sips the tea and grimaces immediately: it's still too hot.

'You'll see... it's round about here... the good thing with writing about something that happened so many years ago – you see, here it is – is that, as so much time has passed it allows one to... focus on the things you want to say. I mean, to specify the memory of the associated events, you know? Here, all yours.'

The woman has sat down in an armchair. She once again moves the mug towards her lips and blows inside to cool the liquid down quicker. She's barefoot and is wearing a loose-fitting t-shirt and a pair of white knickers. Her feet are pretty and tanned, still inviting you to nibble on them every now and then, despite their being almost forty years old. Her left foot dances, and the corresponding ankle is adorned with a thin bracelet of four or five broken threads that yesterday she wore on her wrist. It makes her look younger than she really is. She listens carefully to the beginning of the poem and, judging by her face, she seems to like it.

"Passing in front of a small shop that sold
cheap and flimsy merchandise for workers,
he saw a face inside, a figure
that compelled him to go in, and he pretended
he wanted to look at some coloured handkerchiefs.
He asked about the quality of the handkerchiefs..."

The woman smiles, perhaps wondering if this strategy is more commonly used by girls than boys. Men don't know how to make detours; they go straight to where they want to go and, even then, they are often left behind, whether it's a physical place or the heart of woman.

Slurping on her tea, she interrupts the rhapsody:

'I bet the poem's called Colourful Scarves,' she says.

The man is clearly annoyed by the untimely interruption.

'You've just lost one of your beautiful fingers. Which one do you want me to lop off? One you don't use that often, perhaps… Come on, let me finish reading without interruptions.'

'It wasn't an interruption,' replies the woman. 'It was an intervention.' Seeing the man's face, she immediately apologises, bringing her hands together as if she were praying.

The man goes back to the verse he'd reached when his wife interrupted him and continues.

"He asked about the quality of the handkerchiefs
and how much they cost, his voice choking,
almost silenced by desire…"

He now pauses to breathe in, unsure whether it's emotion or just many hours of work. Like the customer the poem, he too chokes, but for other reasons. The man reads the next three verses before reaching the last part:

"They kept on talking about the merchandise –
but the only purpose: that their hands might touch
over the handkerchiefs, that their faces, their lips,
might move close together as though by chance –
a moment's meeting of limb against limb.

Quickly, secretly, so the shopkeeper sitting at the back
wouldn't realize what was going on."

He pauses, indicating the end of the reading. The woman puts her mug on the floor and claps timidly.

'You've told me about this poem before, haven't you?' she smiles as she says this, but within she laments the fact that, with him, she has never had the opportunity to experience a relationship in which these verses were so necessary. She feels a little hurt. When she met the writer, the man was already tired of decorating his display cabinets with shiny trophies and adorning his vases with bouquets of flowers. He took six tablets a day. He had stopped teaching a few years before. He was still yet to taste success with his own literature, but he made his living talking about other people's books.

'Oh yes,' says the man. 'More than once. He has had a great influence on me!'

'And how old were you back then?'

'It's written here. Exactly twenty-five years old. An eternity ago!'

In her head, the woman recreates that which she has never known: the scene about a boy, a girl, and an old woman in a market. She is still in love. At times she has even remembered certain scenes that she thought might have happened, with the writer as the protagonist. They have never happened, but her imagination dwells on them all the same, creating strange, deceitful memories.

'But,' she insists, 'the end of the poem really does ring a bell…'

The man goes back to it.

'This bit? "Quickly, secretly, so the shopkeeper sitting at the back / wouldn't realize what was going on."'

'Yes, that bit. You've read that to me before, haven't you?'

The man thinks, repeating the question to himself, as he tries to find the part of the poem that takes him back to another one – in this sense, recalling a part of a text seems a lot easier than trying to recall a melody. At least for him, someone who makes his living by writing. He isolates the part of the text required in order to clear up the woman's doubt: "Quickly, secretly, so the shopkeeper sitting at the back / wouldn't realize what was going on". Ah yes, of course. How could he not have recognised one of his most loved poems that he has recited at one time or another to the old lady's granddaughter?

The house was next to an old papermill in which the woman, Francesca, had lived for more than three decades of married life. When I set foot in it for the first time, the new house was a little over twenty years old. She'd had it built without consulting her husband who, grumbling and insolent, had considered it to be an expensive, unnecessary business. Their previous life in the mill was a closed, windowless affair that took place daily under the concrete flooring, with humidity running down the ever damp walls, except when it was hot, like sweat on human skin. The elderly Francesca had told me many times about the physical sensation wrought by the humidity, the constant damp heat that passed through the iciness of the walls against which family furniture had been pushed, or the still colder bathroom where a mirror had once hung for some many years, reflecting her smile and dreams of youth. Nothing but the squat body of a wood-burning stove and its accompanying flue, that travelled up and out of the room like a dark, vertical branch, would bring warmth to the skin and soul. The subterranean house had only one window. As the shutters didn't close properly, it needed to be barred from the inside and nobody had ever thought to repair it to keep out the cold and the rainwater that dripped down into the dining room from the outside. On the days when heavy rain beat at the window, a thin curtain of water would find its way in and they would have to shore up the frame with a folded towel so as to soak it up. And that despite the fact that there were two more floors above their heads, the rotten wooden beams of which would absorb the rivulets of rainwater so they wouldn't drip down onto the fabric of the rugs or bedspreads.

'It was a rat's paradise,' she would say. 'And the ceilings, so very high, were impossible to keep clean! The musty smell of decay was everywhere. In winter, it was the North Pole; in summer we suffered the heat of a thousand devils. And when it rained, merciful God Himself cried in the house.'

She had told me so many times that I had formed a clear, faithful image of the whole scene in my mind's eye, aided by occasional visits to the place. The basement of the mill was gloomy, and though it was by then used only as a storage space for items from the adjacent factory – dried, stale leather straps, worn out through years of use; rusty metal drums; toothed wheels and other items of waste metal – the cold feeling it had brought on, so many decades before, stayed with me. Brambles pushed their way through the gratings of glassless windows, as if eager to claim and spread within the shelter, looming ghosts in a strange and gloomy greenhouse.

Using her own ancient savings, she got in touch with an architect and told him the kind of house she wanted. They would use the land to the south of the old mill, just in front of a linden tree that had been planted by her father-in-law before he had died some two years earlier. One evening before the celebration of Saint John, Francesca cut several flowering branches from the linden with a pair of pruning scissors before leaving them scattered across the windscreens of the five or six cars parked in the courtyard in front of the house. There had been no storm to break branches and blow dead leaves across the windscreens and the night was calm; the bonfire we had set alight was settling down into a bed of red embers and ash. There was no wind to blow the flames, and they had danced upright like cypress trees. The sky, magnificent with its constellations, had threatened rain, and the moon was like a thin slice of melon in the heavens. The older children were trying to jump over the fire. One or two fireworks continued to burst in the darkness, and a dog from a neighbouring farmhouse demonstrated his discontent at the pops of gunpowder that accompanied the party by barking with an irritation that slowly turned into desperation. It wasn't the wind, or even the airy arms of the storm, but rather a hidden hand that brought us the linden flowers. I took the sprig that I had been given and, on reaching home, placed it into the same vase as the dry, blue eucalyptus, there on the table in the entrance to the house. I could have lit a lamp on the table and the effect would have been the same. Francesca had also given me the eucalyptus wreath, long since bereft of its perfume. The first thing you saw when you walked into my house was a vase full of greenery, the combination of the yellow linden flowers and the eucalyptus leaves being fruit of a secret harmony – like the link between some human physiognomies and those of particular breeds of dog, comparing a person's cranial lines and facial features to those of their four-legged friends: a happy sad expression, drooping eyelids, a straight nose, the tapering mouth reminding you of an ever drooling muzzle.

I now live in this ancient house having escaped from another in the centre of the same town and which was cursed by leaks. Not two or three, no; seven or eight. Merciful God cried living teardrops there and the light was less generous and kind than it is here. In just a few years, I have lived in seven or eight different places. In hindsight, the only place that could perhaps be considered home was Francesca's house. We renovated the flat underneath hers, a second-floor place with a terrace that looked out over the river.

Close to the house was a canal that used to carry water from the river up to the family factory when it was still operating full time. So that water would flow there, it had to be brought up via a rotten wooden lock that would earnestly raise it up thanks to a rusty axle that ran a kind of wheel. By turning the stiff wheel, the sluice would creak open and the river water would run off into the canal. The canal bed would have to be cleaned out every year to remove the mud that accumulated there. Likewise, every year it was necessary to cut back the herbaceous nightmare that grew along its edges.

The soft, lilting music of the passing water accompanied our summer nights. The five night workers made rolls of corrugated cardboard but we heard nothing of their work, of their curses aimed at the thick, tiresome paste. Even their presence went unnoticed because the new factory was hidden behind the enormous bulk of the old one. We would sit on the stones that encircled the towering linden tree and if it was still in flower and would take pleasure in the perfume that the breeze would waft around us. My children, still very young, loved to sit there. Francesca would wear an apron, and my son would ask her to tell him again the story of the fox. For the children, the thin channel of water must have looked the same as a distant river. To an active imagination, the pine needles that fell into the water there looked like half-sunken wooden ships. To a child, an oak leaf floating in the water is a full sail, cut free from the rope that tied it to the mast and stern.

'The story is too frightening for this time of night,' said Francesca, 'and your sister won't be able to sleep.'

I carried the little girl piggyback around my neck as she furiously protested and whirled her arms around trying to and break free of my grip. She wanted to hear again, under the clear stars, the disturbing story of the fox trapped in a watery snare and she wasn't going to take no for an answer.

Up in my children's bedroom, I opened the window that looked out on the space presided over by the linden. Apart from the cats rubbing themselves up against their legs, my son and his great-grandmother were alone. She didn't skip a single detail of the story and the boy's eyes shone wide like the moon. I only picked up a few sparse words. Brightly lit moths fluttered around the thick, yellow light hanging from the front. My daughter was restless. I often whispered delicate lullabies to her with terrible lyrics such as: 'our little girl, the Angel of Sleep will come and sew your eyelids shut'. So young was she that the next day I would help her rub away the Angel of Sleep's leftover thread from her eyes.

She guessed that the story had already got to the part where, at a midday during a hot July, a factory worker dipped his bare feet in the canal and one of them brushed up against something that was like touching a wooden post covered in herbs and dead leaves or a well-worn step. Surprised at the size of the thing, the man pulled his feet out of the water and lay face down, swapping his feet for his hands and splashed around in the canal trying to pull out the submerged branch, or whatever it was, that intrigued him so much. The grandmother measured out the length of the canal and that which had brushed up against the worker's foot with wild hand gestures.

In order to sleep my daughter required a glass of warm water though I'm not sure if she ever swallowed a single drop. But her lips were refreshed by the liquid: a pure water that her great-grandmother would bring up from her private well. And only after this would she set her head down on her pillow and try to sleep.

The precarious, sunken stepping stone in the canal was actually the body of a fox that had fallen in there a few weeks before. With his hands protected by his leather gloves, the man touched the bony body that was hardly able to oppose the flow of the water running over it. The current had already carried away the fetid stench and had washed the body clean. The man lifted it out of the water and it was only then that he realised what the horrible dripping bag of bones was that he had in his hands. Old Francesca, complying with the demands of the listener, gave all manner of details about the discovery. Cats and rats had fallen into the canal, but it was the first time that a fox had been pulled out. Its eyes were gone, and its paws were but bones partially covered in flesh.

My children have been educated in the harsh school of nature and they are not as afraid of these things as perhaps might be a child less *au fait* with life in the countryside and the prickle of sensations that we get from being amongst trees. For example: under a crunching branch; on the muddy banks of a river overflowing after a heavy downpour; touching the corpse of a dog in the middle of a goat path; or, the bark of a pine tree covered in sticky drops of resin and infested with ants fighting to survive. I see their love – or perhaps altruistic passion – for Mother Earth when they pick up a cat by the scruff of its neck, with the same solicitude or naturalness as its own mother, or when they press a new-born rabbit to their chest, cradling it in their arms, as smooth as a soft cotton blanket. They have taught me how a goat's heart beats. Me, as clumsy as any when it comes to the small wonders of the natural world. Now that they are older they keep a vegetable garden and laden me with lettuce, strawberries, onions and tomatoes and I take them all back home happy to transfer some of the soul of their garden to my city fridge. My son's hands smell of the earth. He works alone, deciding what to plant between one row and the other. A little while ago his sister showed me a baby bird in a shoebox with a bed of withered cabbage leaves acting as its makeshift nest. The injured chick had fallen out of a tree like a lost ball and my daughter, feeding it with a syringe, told me it was a great tit. It opened its beak and the syringe shot skimmed milk into its mouth. Unfortunately, far from its mother the bird died some five days later despite the prodigious attention it was afforded. But the tenderness my daughter shows towards animals and the handiness of my son, with his hat and armed with a bow that is almost as tall as he is, ready to go out to shoot his arrows at the wild boar that run riot in his vegetable garden… they have learnt all of this from their great-grandmother. They owe it all to her, this splendid moral heritage touching the very beating heart of life!

The man extends his arms. He doesn't now take as many pills, and he feels moderately better, sometimes even a certain euphoria that is by no means pathological. He doesn't suffer from the brusque mood swings like the years before. He tires more easily when he writes but this is most likely due to his age. The woman is always with him. He doesn't like it when she hangs clothes out while he works and he has dropped more than a couple of hints, even asking her directly to leave.

He rereads the sentence that, when he wrote it half an hour before seemed to him very suggestive but that now seems too heavy with metaphor. Does the sentence howl? He carries on as he knows that the atmosphere he has to create around the old house is key to the story. He doesn't want to stop here. The bedroom is hot because a little while earlier he turned off the air conditioning. A few minutes go by and he hears only the tapping of the keyboard and the rustle of the pages of a magazine the woman is slowly reading. The tapping is uneven: the man writes a few lines, carried away on the magic of the words or his passion for what he is writing. He remembers situations and recreates them on the screen. He stops suddenly, thinks for a few seconds, and goes back. He corrects. He concludes that a sentence, set amongst the others, is not completely lost, and is blessed with a certain metaphorical weight.

The woman turns her page quickly, followed by one and then another… and only then, on the last page, does she spend five or six minutes reading it from the first to the last line: the photos on it, clearly more immodest than the others, catch her eye and with three fingers on her absorbed, engrossed right hand she bends back the pages, flicking the pages under her thumb like we have seen bankers do so many times with wads of freshly printed banknotes. Perhaps it's the Sunday section detailing someone's biography, or part of their biography, telling the reader the very wildest parts of their life. Not so much a frivolous, bohemian artist, but rather a radical experimenter. The woman stares at it. She doesn't like what she is seeing or what she is reading but she can't help herself. The repulsive images feature nine bowls of goat's blood with different things floating in each one. In the first are cereals; in the others, sliced apples, biscuits, and some breadsticks. In the last one lie dark genitals and the metal from some dental braces.

The man stands up and opens the window and the noise from the street quickly invades the bedroom. He thinks about the quality of the windows and how well they keep the sound out: double glazed, hermetically sealed. He's grateful for them.

'I think I owe you an apology,' says the man. 'That thing from before… I was a little insolent.'

She shrugs her shoulders and he doesn't know if she is forgiving him or giving him up as a lost cause. But of course, she forgives him. She wouldn't have spent this long with him otherwise. It is clear she is still in love with him.

'It's just that when I write, I lose track of things. Like when I read something out loud. Please, can you read this part and let me know your honest opinion?'

He points at the screen with his right index finger and urges her to read down the page.

'Here?'

'No, from here. Yes, this bit.'

The woman starts to read:

'The soft, lilting music of the passing water.' She stops at: 'the very beating heart of life.'

Outside, the sound of a rubbish truck following its route around the city reaches up even to the heights of the block of flats. Stopping, the sound of the mechanism swallowing binbags full of rubbish can be heard. The stink of the rubbish – an identical smell no matter where you are in the world – wafts up into the man's study.

The woman is focussed on the text.

'Do you like it?' he asks her.

'Yes, I do. But is it all true, what you're writing? Was she really like that?'

'In a story,' he replies, 'everything, absolutely everything is true. Didn't you know? The moment you tell it, it becomes real, and not only that, it becomes true. It all ends up as being true.'

'It's as if you are mostly interested in stories about families. Or stories about individuals, like that one about the man who was a teacher and who is discovered by the protagonist, some twenty years later, in a restaurant. Well, I'm not sure how to describe it. It's as if… well, of course, it's impossible to tell someone's whole life. I suppose you could say that you write about family episodes, or individual episodes, but placing more emphasis on the symbolic side of things, right?'

The writer says that he'd never thought about it that way, but he likes the woman's theory. The fox's corpse represents life's struggles. Is that what the woman meant about the symbolic side of things? And the slice of watermelon? What a strange, almost sexual, thing to do and all just for a piece of fruit! If only it were as easy to strip other parts of our lives back to the bone so as to poke around and manage.

'Look at the phrase I've just come across in this magazine!' Now it's the woman's turn to take the initiative in the conversation. 'It's from a bizarre photo: "I have had a life as fake as a mannequin's pregnancy." Weird, right?'

Rather than weird, he considers it to be dramatic. But he recognises that at some time or another, when passing in front of a clothes shop for pregnant women, he has felt something similar to that which the phrase is trying to say. All mannequins are fake, as are all dolls, puppets and all figures, whether idealistic or grotesque. And when they take on a pregnant form, even more so. They have no sex, but they fill an empty space in life.

I had the overwhelming certainty of seeing the first symptom of my friend's memory loss the day I asked her about her plans for the coming summer.

I was hoping to persuade her to join us on a Sunday outing.

'Francesca, you need a change of scenery. We'll take the car and head down to the reservoir. There aren't the mosquitos there were a few years ago and they've sealed off the rubbish tip that kicked up such a smell. We could take a picnic for lunch. What do you think? Potato omelette, some cuts of meat and a bota of cold white wine! We could take a paddle. You wouldn't have to worry about anything; I'll take care of it all.'

She said she wasn't in the mood. She said that all there was left for her to do was die and that only then would her work be done. She smiled as she said it with conviction, as if her work needed to be sealed shut with a smile, like so many other, far less morbid things she had experienced in the last few years of her life.

Despite her advanced age, I felt she was still due to experience a few more important things. My children were growing up and they spoke to her in that same indulgent tone they used to address children younger than them who were just starting to understand certain expressions. They spoke loudly or close to her ear because her hearing had deteriorated of late.

'You have so much left to see,' I said. 'I hope you live to see one hundred...' She flicked her hand back as if to bat the responsibility back my way. 'One hundred years old, oh yes. We'll celebrate for a whole week... you might even say that all you are yet to experience is as round and unknown as a watermelon, and as sweet and delicious as slice of watermelon when you're thirsty. You remember when I first started coming here, years ago, you would do me the honour of letting me cut the season's first slice of watermelon?

She said no, she didn't remember it, and that she had never been very fond of watermelon. She preferred cherries and peaches, both of which were easier to carry around and eat. For many years she had used her apron as a bag to collect the pips; the only bag she always had handy when she went out for a walk because she didn't take it off until it was time to go to bed. She would come back having picked berries or figs or picked up an injured bird from the ground or even stones and scraps of bark she found delicate or suggestive. While her mouth was still healthy and had all its teeth she would bite down on the hot peaches, freshly picked from the tree, without bothering to peel them.

For me, that was the first sign, like the first spot of rust on the iron bar of a gate, high up on top of a cliff, enduring salt from the sea and the rubbing of a thousand hands. But the rust spreads; the spot gets bigger. It was the first sign, yes, and it stuck in my mind like the sharp pointed knife would stick into the shining skin of the watermelon so many years before. I would drive it in deep to cut out a triangle and hand it over to the lady of the house.

'Delicious,' she would say. 'You can start cutting up the rest.' Watermelon, along with peaches, figs, cherries, and apricots, was her favourite. But if she had to choose one, if someone had made her choose, then it would have been watermelon. We would eat them throughout the summer and now she didn't remember, despite my telling her all about the times we had eaten watermelon on warm summer evenings and short, sweet stories like the one about the girl who, with a badly cut piece of watermelon in hand, peppered with seeds, pretended to eat some troubadour's ant-infested heart. Or another about the very young boy who made a toy sailing ship out of a piece of watermelon skin using ice lolly sticks for the masts and made sails out of paper napkins. And now she didn't remember but claimed that she had never cared much for watermelon saying that only cherries or peaches had ever made her mouth water.

With lunch finished, I collected up the crumbs from the tablecloth as I went through her memories, both happy and sad, along with morsels of images still not yet forgotten. I pushed them over to the edge of the table where my other hand was waiting to take charge of the scraps that Francesca would run off into her apron pocket before emptying them out, to the joy of the sparrows. In posh restaurants, waiters come over before dessert and use some shiny metal tool to gather up the bothersome grains. Running the little metal tool across the table, they remove the breadcrumbs, which tend to get stuck on the sleeves of woollen jumpers, before serving exquisite chocolate or cheeses and bringing coffee to the table which is dressed in a whiter than white tablecloth. That is, of course, if you haven't let slip a few drops of wine, leaving a violet stain.

A long after-dinner conversation in July a few years ago now comes to mind. She was still able to name all the mill owners in the area and to explain the history of the country with all the twists and turns that you'd expect: the family betrayals and political wheeling and dealing. And she still remembered the names of those who had accompanied her father as he fled to France, with the fascists from neighbouring villages in hot pursuit. She even described their faces and told us the nicknames of each of the houses they came from. The sun had gone down behind the rooftiles as it wound down for the afternoon. With the window looking out onto the magnolia with its varnished leaves and, a few metres further away, the majestic linden, the summer afternoon light was sweet. Inside the house, the heat and our full tummies made us deliciously sleepy. We spoke of many things including some that I already knew because she'd repeated them many times before. Hours passed. On the table was an open newspaper that I'd started to read but had immediately given up in order to listen with curiosity to her stories. And there was a cup of coffee with a spoon inside like the clapper of a bell. On the sofa lay a scratched guitar that I'd used to play the few songs I knew, practising combinations of the few chords that so often died away in poorly defined, anodyne tones.

'I didn't want to upset you,' she said, apologetically, but all I could think about was that once she was gone I would lose forever the possibility of not only speaking to her, but also the opportunity to listen to a fascinating person, the most fascinating I had ever met, and I had no desire to waste a single moment at her side. Some nights, after dinner, we would lie back in a pair of sun loungers on her terrace and, smoking a cigar with my children eating minty sweets, we would let loose our conscientious observations of the stars. If you focussed enough on them, you could feel a little vertigo. She would tell us stories about her youth and, one at a time, we would ask her to repeat some chapter from her life that had grabbed our attention, had made us laugh or moved us in some way.

'Don't move, I'll be right back,' she would say and she would stand up and head down to the clearing in front of the house with a bowl full of breadcrumbs that trembled meekly in a little milk for five or six cats to fight over. The river in front of the house that played host to the sounds of ducks playing by day was then quiet, barely a current of mysterious water, running along sadly or wearily, as if suffering from the intense heat and the parched earth might suck it all dry, leaving on its apocalyptic banks the dried corpses of the last of the carps.

In mid-September we would accompany her across the bridge to a vineyard we had, and from the vines we would pick the little hidden berries, bound tightly by tendrils, that the harvesters had forgotten to take a couple of weeks before. They were the sweetest ones because they had received the bonus of a few more days of sun.

'They're the hunters' grapes,' she would say. 'Their dessert for after their sandwiches.'

She always carried a Swiss penknife in her apron pocket and would tell us about her ancient world of harvesting-tools and equipment. I had taken part in a couple of harvests, many summers before, unlike my children. Francesca called the heavy leaves dragging across the earth 'seasonal clothes' and, turning to her great-grandchildren, she would tell them a story about the circle of life in that vineyard that, dispossessed of all its fruit and its leaves rusted, would soon transform itself into an autumn garden of cardboard leaves. She would ask them, tiny like rabbits, to imagine themselves in the middle of a forest of vines.

'Around the day of Saint Joseph's, the weather will make the vines cry again, and each one will produce a little tear, and another and a third, and then some more, and they'll roll down the trunk and the sap will be renewed. And all will grow again, and you will see it again, and the vines will burst once again with leaves and, finally, grapes.'

Yes, the grapes would swell once again like clusters of translucent green beads and on the celebration of the Mother of God in August the groups of harvest workers would come once again, darker in skin with every passing year. One of those days, the woman grabbed hold of a vine and I remember that it caught my attention. She pulled it up as if trying to rip it out of the soil, but the roots' long years of burrowing deep had forged strong anchors in the earth and the woman's own years had weakened her. How she loved her land! And by describing it to us in such detail, it became precise, necessary knowledge.

'And the harvesters' hands, as they work, are always sticky and every now and then a wasp finds itself attracted to the sugar on their skin. And then, well! They run off to make mud by peeing on the soil before spreading it well over the little red blister. When I was young, every harvest worker would protect their head with a handkerchief. And we would wait until after Sunday lunch before dancing the nights away at the local village parties.'

Evermore will we miss her lessons on natural and human history!

Early one evening, arriving back at home, a dripping hose had formed a dark stain on the floor in front of the garage door. Two or three thirsty wasps were refreshing themselves there and refused to move out of the way while drowsily buzzing around my children's ankles as they went by to get their bicycles. Summer has always been the children's favourite season.

When does a person die? If they lose a good part of their memory can we consider them to be less alive?

Apart from the memory lapses and her numerous repetitions, Francesca lived a normal life for a woman of her age. She still collected flowers. She wasn't allowed to drive anymore. She walked often, but always with someone keeping an eye on her so that she didn't go too far and get lost. She maintained her agility.

She would often fall over, but in a dismissive tone she would insist that she had always fallen over things and that it had nothing to do with her age. If her face ever hit the ground – something that, unfortunately, wasn't uncommon – a black eye would spread out across her face, the bruise expanding over her cheek and, her blood surprised by the accident, would stain her cheek blue down to her lips and two days later turn a yellow colour like ripe quince. Despite so many falls she claimed never to have broken any part of what she called 'the flow chart of bones in my body'. Occasionally she would cut herself in the kitchen and her granddaughter would soak bandages in alcohol – Francesca no longer remembered where the first aid box was – before squeezing the wound tight.

'I have always scabbed over well,' she would say. 'This is nothing.'

A rosary of blood drops would be left across the tiles that her carer Juana would clean off the next day.

When do we die, and are we dead before the doctor certifies our passing?

I thought many times of the celebrated couplets that Manrique dedicated to his deceased father. How I'd like to "remember the sleeping soul", but just sleeping, not dead – poets are ever dealing

with metaphors. And to bring up my obsession with memory, as if
the woman could follow me and as if it might help her:

'Do you remember, Francesca, how we met one Sunday in
November at a market some fifteen years ago and you were wearing
a green coat? Yes, green. And a knitted bag.'

'No, I don't. Fifteen years ago, already? Well I never!'

I go back to her house and she isn't there. Her daughter has gone
with her to her Thursday afternoon Memory Workshop. I sit down
on a chair in the dining room and look at the table where we've
eaten lunch together so many times waiting for the cuckoo clock to
mark the hour, but I realise that the weights are dead and the chains
no longer move. When was the last time the whistling bird opened
its door? Time stands still. The oilskin on the table is stained by a
dark, circular mark from when the cafetière had burned it. There is
another coffee stain, more recent and still sticky. I examine a photograph taken by her granddaughter, the mother of my children: it's of
the woman standing in the middle of a field of red poppies. The old
shrunken plants reach up to her waist and seem to be in desperate
need of watering. In her hand is a poppy and she is holding it out
towards the camera. Perhaps the girl had asked her to and so she
holds it out as an offering. Perhaps, by the time we get to the flower,
it has lost its colour and fragile petals. She no longer cares for the
plants or the flowers. It is now a task for the younger ones.

Next to the telephone and a shelf full of books and paintings
in the office, I see a piece of paper stuck to the wall with a few
phone numbers written on it, including my own. Next to it is my
name written in her clear but slightly shaky handwriting. From the
window the linden tree is out of view. Down the hall is the room
where my children slept for a few years before we renovated the flat
below. I think of the summer evenings when the boy and his great-

grandmother would sit together at the foot of the linden tree. It was back when the family factory was still active and the canal was full of water. The magnolia was yet to suffer from the disease that killed it and forced us to cut it down. I open the window and the linden tree is still there, firm.

I go back to the office. There is a framed photo of her father at the Tolosa train station in 1939. The writing on it is in Spanish. She was only seventeen years old. I read the spines of the books on the shelf. I pull one out and leaf through it. I put it back again. I pull another one out and open it. They are worthless; many of them have been stamped with blue ink that says they were given away as part of a bank promotion. A piece of paper falls out of this second book and I immediately recognise my children's mother's handwriting. The page contains two handwritten poems that I must have recited to her over the telephone at some time or another. I continue to read, but there's no need: I know these verses off by heart. I am moved to think that one day, many years ago, the telephone rang in the girl's grandmother's house. Back then there were no mobiles or email. The telephone rang and someone was waiting for the call while someone else, quite aware of who was phoning, busied herself in the welcoming winter kitchen. Soup was boiling away in a sauce-pan. It was evening and the two women were alone. On the marble worktop was a plate with some cuts of meat waiting to be breaded. When could it have been? The end of October? It might have been November. I hadn't been to the house yet, though it wouldn't be long. I try to remember how I imagined the place before setting foot in it. I desist. Outside, it was cold. The ground, covered with fallen oak leaves, runs down to a path along the back of the building. I was the one reading a poem on the other end of the line, a poem about two boys who, eyes ablaze, embraced against the wall of the allotment, "Quickly, so nobody would see." The words are faithful to that moment from so many years ago. The poem starts with the words: "I perfectly remember". But did the memory have any chance of manifesting itself perfectly? Is there anything we can claim to remember clearly? I put the piece of paper in my pocket.

The last time I was with her, some two weeks ago, I'd bumped into her walking close to the house along the path to the allotments, and the field of corn a little further away. There is a bridge crossing a river. On the other side of the river is a meadow and, if you follow the path along, the waterworks. From here you can see the village. You can only make out one of the cemetery's white walls, topped by a turret as if it were a castle.

She was wandering alone, without anyone to watch out for her, and she was carrying a bunch of flowers in her hand. That image of her was touched by a certain delicate mystery. She called out my name: she always recognised me. She asked me something and I answered her two or three times. The woman didn't hear properly and dropped her head. She laughed. I thought back to the first time I had found myself under scrutiny from her eyes. Or that same first time I had surrendered to the charm of her smile.

Arriving home, I knew that everything that was to be fitted in between the Christmas gift of eucalyptus leaves and the flowering sprig from the linden tree one summer solstice, had happened. The bunch, though not yet funerary, was dried out. In just a few months, my old friend had grown more and more absent. I started to write a story called: "The Eucalyptus Leaves and the Linden Tree Sprig."

In the end, I kept only the linden tree. Perhaps because, though cut by an unwell hand, the dry flowers that crumbled away on my bedside table symbolised for me the beauty of her soul: the most generous I have ever had the privilege of knowing. I then had a title and a first sentence: "The last time I was with her." Though I'd leave it until the end. I opened a bottle of red wine from a good year and poured myself out a glass, ready to enjoy it as I started my story. The woman would be luminous yet wounded, laughing and cheerful, and the beginning would be sad, and though unavoidably melancholy, unconfutable. No, it would be better to begin my short story with an exordium and leave the ending for another time. Either way, I finished writing the paragraph and signed it off with a final sentence that was less funerary than hopeful. A few weeks later, I'd have time to decide if it was to be the last sentence in the paragraph, or the whole story:

In her relative unconsciousness, with the bunch of flowers in her hand – flowers still warm from the sun – you would have said she was entirely happy.